FUJINO OMORI
ILLUSTRATION BY
NIRITSU
CHARACTER DESIGN BY
SUZUHITO YASUDA
“Please stop teasing me, Syr.”
IS IT WRONG TO TRY TO PICK UP GIRLS IN A DUNGEON?
FAMILIA CHRONICLE
Episode Lyu
© NIRITSU

CONTENTS

FUJINO OMORI

ILLUSTRATION BY
NIRITSU

CHARACTER DESIGN BY
SUZUHITO YASUDA

IS IT WRONG TO TRY TO PICK UP GIRLS IN A DUNGEON?
FAMILIA CHRONICLE: Episode Lyu
FUJINO OMORI

Translation by Dale DeLucia
Cover art by NIRITSU

This book is a work of fiction. Names, characters, places, and incidents are the product of the author's imagination or are used fictitiously. Any resemblance to actual events, locales, or persons, living or dead, is coincidental.

Original Japanese edition published in 2017 by SB Creative Corp.
This English edition is published by arrangement with SB Creative Corp., Tokyo in care of Tuttle-Mori Agency, Inc., Tokyo.

Yen On
1290 Avenue of the Americas
New York, NY 10104

Visit us at yenpress.com
facebook.com/yenpress
twitter.com/yenpress
yenpress.tumblr.com
instagram.com/yenpress

First Yen On Edition: June 2018

Yen On is an imprint of Yen Press, LLC.
The Yen On name and logo are trademarks of Yen Press, LLC.

Library of Congress Cataloging-in-Publication Data
Names: Ōmori, Fujino, author. | Niritsu, illustrator. | Yasuda, Suzuhito, designer. | DeLucia, Dale, translator.
Title: Is it wrong to try to pick up girls in a dungeon? familia chronicle episode Lyu / Fujino Omori ; illustration by Niritsu ; character design by Suzuhito Yasuda ; translation by Dale DeLucia.
Other titles: Dungeon ni deai wo motomeru no wa machigatteirudarouka familia chronicle episode Ryu. English | Episode Ryu
Description: First Yen On edition. | New York : Yen On, June 2018.
Identifiers: LCCN 2018006599 | ISBN 9780316448253 (paperback)
Subjects: CYAC: Fantasy. | Kidnapping—Fiction. | Adventure and adventurers—Fiction.
Classification: LCC PZ7.1.O54 It 2018 | DDC [Fic]—dc23
LC record available at https://lccn.loc.gov/2018006599

ISBNs: 978-0-316-44825-3 (paperback)
978-0-316-44826-0 (ebook)

10 9 8 7 6 5 4 3 2 1

LSC-C

Printed in the United States of America

FUJINO OMORI
ILLUSTRATION BY **NIRITSU**
CHARACTER DESIGN BY **SUZUHITO YASUDA**

CRUSH THE GRAND CASINO!

1

"The Benevolent Mistress? No way. Why even go to a place like that?"

In the corner of a dark, dismal tavern, a grimy-looking human man sat at a small round table drinking cheap ale.

"The place has great food and booze for sure, plus the staff are real easy on the eyes, but it's expensive—and if you start any kind of trouble, you'll get tossed out in an instant and wind up at the healer's."

The surrounding patrons' voices were low and gruff. Amid the din of rowdy laughs and shouts, the man was sitting on a creaky old chair as he always was.

"...Huh? Did you ask who'll thrash you? That's obvious, isn't it? The girls who work there!"

He grabbed one of the dried pieces of meat from his plate and tore into it. Chewing loudly, the man with a new scar on his face half smiled.

"That's not a place for small fries like us. Especially considering that dwarf mistress; words can't even describe how scary she is."

He took another swig from his mug to hide a shudder. The chatter of the other drinking patrons got louder, swelling like a wave. Drinking like he was trying to dunk his face in his ale, the man suddenly smiled as his cheeks reddened.

"But you know...if you're ever looking for help wherever you can, and really, truly, have a problem...buy a drink there and try crying into it..."

When someone asked why, the man wiped his mouth and responded, "Because *she's* there. Even compared to the other ridiculous workers at that shop, it's terrifying how strong she is. The woman is way too serious, insanely demanding, and as beautiful as a real fairy…"

As he trailed off, he suppressed his smile. His shoulders shook, as if laughing in scorn—or perhaps trembling in fear—then he lifted his head and whispered so low that it seemed no one else would be able to hear him.

"She's a strange elf in Orario who still holds on to some sense of justice. If you ever get wrapped up in something dangerous, go check it out. She might help you…"

The man left it at that and raised his mug again, drowning himself in his cheap ale.

2

In a certain city district, the moon had already set, but there was still no trace of the sun. A flurry of wind could be heard in the early dawn. The high-pitched gusts sounded over and over, trembling in the air for a moment like a birdcall or a reed pipe before the darkness returned to silence.

A slender elf woman was swinging a wooden sword nearly as long as she was tall. Her movements were swift and sharp as her elegant arms whipped the sword from overhead straight down with impeccable form. An instant later, she reversed the edge, slicing diagonally upward with a speed rivaling any quick-draw technique. If she were in an actual fight, her opponent would probably have run away in the face of such deft skill.

Her dyed, pale green hair swayed as her sword flashed. She wore a light tunic and short pants that fluttered when she moved. Her fair skin stood out under the dark sky.

"...Is it time?"

The sound of one last, particularly sharp practice swing echoed as the elf—Lyu Leon—finished her morning practice.

Inside the giant city walls, her eyes narrowed once the sun started to reveal itself in the eastern sky. Her body glistened with a thin sheen of sweat as the early morning air cleared.

This was the Labyrinth City, Orario. It was a well-known metropolis that prospered as the Center of the World, sitting atop the only underground dungeon in the world. Lyu was employed at one of the taverns in the city, The Benevolent Mistress.

She was an early riser. The restaurant's preparations started early in the morning, but she swung her wooden sword in the dark every day well before that, when the sun had yet to climb above the horizon. Even as a former adventurer who had washed her hands of delving into the Dungeon, Lyu was still meticulous in her training.

Perhaps it was because the elf warrior had found herself in peril several times since she had arrived in Orario, but regardless, she had not forgotten to be diligent in her studies.

Frankly, one should pursue self-improvement and similar ideals until they become habit.

The tavern's courtyard was wide, surrounded by wooden structures not connected to the main building. Originally there were plans for another expansion, so the area had been cleared out and part of the ground was paved with stones. The shop's outdoor storage shed was also in the courtyard. Already sweaty, Lyu looked down at her slender arms.

"This isn't enough..."

Her true feelings unconsciously escaped from her lips in a whisper. Once, she had invited her coworkers, who were plenty strong themselves, but they refused to come a second time. Apparently, she had not controlled herself enough. They had called her a training junkie and complained that she did not hold back. She was always overdoing it. Remembering the abuse that had been hurled at her in the past, Lyu unconsciously sighed.

"Maybe I should ask Mr. Cranell to join me next time."

Looking up at the slightly dark sky, Lyu thought of a certain adventurer. She had only just gotten to know him—though it had already been two months since they met. He was a young human boy, still wet behind the ears, but he was also making progress at shocking speed, both figuratively and literally. For a number of reasons, he had caught Lyu's eye. *He seems to be working toward some kind of goal himself, so training together could work out well for both of us.*

But after thinking that far, Lyu suddenly shook her head. *No, I couldn't do that to Syr.* The boy was her friend's sweetheart and perhaps even a future lover. Spending her early morning practice alone with him while knowing that would be dishonorable. At least, that was how Lyu felt.

*On the other hand, I don't have any ulterior motives. If it was only training, then…*Her thoughts drifted, but as she imagined Syr's face, a sense of guilt welled up in her heart.

Conflicted, Lyu cleared her mind and headed toward her room among the wooden buildings. First she had to clean herself, then change into her uniform. The sun had already cleared the city wall, and dazzling light was starting to shine on the city as Lyu prepared for another day as a waitress at the tavern.

It was another bustling day at The Benevolent Mistress.

The three-story stone building gave the impression of a tidy little inn that was bigger than it seemed from the outside. Its location on West Main Street made it convenient for customers to come and go.

During the day, the clientele was largely female and consisted primarity of regular city residents, while after dark, the bar and tables were usually filled with adventurers returning from the Dungeon. It managed the different groups of customers well: The menu changed as morning became evening, charging adventurers who had more money to burn with higher prices.

As the restaurant's dwarf owner, Mia Grand, liked to say, "We're treating them to our delicious food and drink, after all. If they can't pay, then they don't get any!"

In reality, a great deal of adventurers were regulars who visited often, many obsessed with her special fruit wine (which was guaranteed to taste amazing).

"The morning is better, though, meow..."

"When it gets late, the beer-starved adventurers swarm us...Ugh, it's depressing, meow."

"Hey, kitties, you're being slow. Mama Mia is going to yell at you."

The former top-tier adventurer Mia had gone into semi-retirement and opened The Benevolent Mistress, where several women lived and worked. Lyu was one of them.

The catgirls leaning on the counter were Ahnya and Chloe, while the human warning them like always was Runoa. Lyu didn't pay them any mind as she carried a fruit tart on a platter.

"Two guests coming in!"

The girl with light blue-gray hair guiding the two new customers was Syr. She was the only employee who didn't room at the tavern. She was a human girl with standout looks; the tavern used her as a cute salesgirl to lure in traffic from the street. Unlike Lyu, who was brusque and difficult to approach, Syr graciously treated everyone equally. She had won the adoration of the male patrons as a straightforward, honest local girl. Even rowdy adventurers who had too much to drink calmed down when confronted with her surprising stubbornness and fearless smile. Thanks to the tavern owner Mia, as well as Lyu and the rest of the employees, The Benevolent Mistress was running smoothly like always.

The inside bustling with demi-human women made for a picturesque sight as sunlight shone through the windows. It was almost noon, and traffic on the street outside was picking up when the shop's moment of peace was shattered.

"Then what? Are you saying you sold Anna?!"

Lyu, the other staff, and all the customers in the tavern glanced over at a human couple Syr had just seated.

"I didn't sell her—she was taken."

"That's the same thing, isn't it, you idiot! That's why I kept telling you to stop gambling..."

The woman with her flaxen hair tied back had seen many years come and go, but she had not lost her beauty. She raised her voice as the man sitting across from her responded listlessly, an unkempt five-o'clock shadow noticeable on his face.

"What kind of father puts his own daughter up as collateral for a bet?!"

The mother shouted one last time before burying her face in her hands and bawling.

An awkward wave of unease swept through the restaurant. Ahnya and Chloe, who were diligently going about their work, peeked their heads out of kitchen at the loud sobs. Runoa stopped in her tracks as she, Lyu, Syr, and the catgirl chefs all exchanged glances.

The middle-aged man noticed all of the gazes focused on their table, and finally looked up as he jumped to his feet, kicking away his chair.

"What are you looking at?! This isn't some spectacle! Just eat your crappy food, assholes!"

"W-wait, stop that!"

The woman tried to hold him back as he flew into a rage, but he would not be subdued. He clenched the glass of water that had been placed in front of him, flinging the contents everywhere. As he continued swinging it around, the customers nearby shrieked, followed by an immediate *thump*—something caught his flailing arm.

"Pardon me, sir, but if you are going to make a scene, could you please pay now and leave instead?"

"What did you—Oww?!"

A sharp cry of pain cut off the question. Runoa had apparently approached without a sound, and she squeezed tighter. She seemed like any other girl her age, but her grip convinced the man his arm was at the breaking point.

"Hey, who do you think cleans this floor, meow?"

"A clown who wastes the food and water we prepared for him can go get cursed by the gods and drop into hell for all I care, meow."

More *thumps* echoed as a wickedly smiling Chloe and a visibly furious Ahnya came up from behind the angry man to grab hold of his shoulders. Then they whipped out one leg each, smoothly tripping their quarry. With his support knocked out from under him, he fell straight the floor.

"Wh…what?"

As soon as he hit the ground, the man's body rose back into the air as the towering dwarf mistress of the establishment grasped him by the collar of his tunic. He was a full-grown man, but she needed only one hand to hold him up. When he saw Mia's dangerous expression up close, all the color drained from his face.

"It's pretty ballsy to call our food bad before you've even had any, don't you think?"

"Aaaahhhh…!!"

"—You're annoying the other customers, you idiot!"

The next instant, she tossed him in a smooth arc through the entryway and halfway into the main street, while the man screamed all the way. A carriage suddenly came to a halt, horse neighing, when the man rolled out of nowhere into the middle of the street. The throng was startled for a moment, but as soon as people recognized what tavern he had flown out of, everyone carefully avoided him and moved along as though they were used to it.

The Benevolent Mistress. It was a place where the women Mia employed all had *special circumstances*, and most were accustomed to fighting.

Adventurers who didn't know better were often drawn in by the tavern's reputation for sweet and beautiful girls. It was a familiar scene in the neighborhood to see customers who made *foolish mistakes* come flying out the door looking the worse for wear.

As the shop calmed down, Lyu thought she had been too slow to react.

"I'm sorry, it sounded like a bit of a distressing story, but…did something happen?"

Syr calmly approached her, head tilted slightly, but the dumbfounded woman froze and was unable to answer.

©-NIRITSU

* * *

"...Gambling with his daughter as collateral..."

Lyu unconsciously furrowed her brow. After collecting the man, who had fainted in the street, she joined Syr in a corner of the tavern to listen to their story.

The woman's name was Karen and her husband's was Huey. They were a couple who made their living day to day in the magic-stone manufacturing business by helping out in a small store. They had lived in the city's western district until that very day—Huey liked to gamble, and had gotten involved in an incident as a result.

"I had no choice...By that point, there wasn't anything I could do. I had to. Why else would I wager my daughter, Anna...?"

After coming to, the battered Huey lifelessly explained the situation as he sat in a chair.

He had somehow ended up wagering the daughter he had raised with Karen as collateral in a gamble—and lost. Lyu, an elf known for her strict standards, couldn't hide the scorn and contempt in her gaze. Syr put her hand on Karen's shoulder to comfort her as she held back tears. Ahnya was shocked, as were the others listening as they went about their work.

"What was so unavoidable? This happened because you were playing with fire—didn't it?!"

"Th-that's...B-but, at first they were saying 'it's just a game.' But when I kept losing, the atmosphere changed all of a sudden! They talked about kicking in the door of our home if it seemed like I couldn't pay up what I lost. One thing led to another, and then I couldn't undo it..."

When he noticed Karen's teary-eyed glare, Huey swallowed the rest of his excuses. From what he had said so far, it was clear he had failed the last big gamble, losing his daughter and his house in the process. Earlier that morning, a bunch of thugs kidnapped his daughter, while Karen, dazed from being thrown out of her home, went to the only place left where she could calm down—The Benevolent Mistress. When she heard the details from Huey, they started bickering, and the rest was obvious.

Huey was talking about waking up with a massive hangover, handcuffed after the party ended, when Syr abruptly asked, "The others involved in this gamble, did they happen to be adventurers?"

"...Yeah, they were a bunch of delinquents from several different familias. They threatened me and wouldn't stop glaring...'If it's a wager for your beloved daughter, then we can give you one last chance...'"

Hearing that, Karen bent over the table, crying again. "You shameless...!"

As her insults came out as sobs, her already hopeless failure of a husband became subdued and bowed his head again and again. However, Lyu's eyebrow rose slightly in surprise. There was one part of the story that did not sit well with her. To be more precise, she had seen an operation that resembled this in the past.

"Your daughter, Anna, could you tell me a bit more about her?"

At her question, both Karen and Huey managed to raise their heads and exchange glances. Gradually, they answered the elf who stood on the other side of the table, staring intensely.

"Well, like I said before, she is my pride and joy..."

"Yes, she is very pretty, like I used to be, and she's good-natured. A little reserved, but she's a good girl."

Just as Huey started, Karen wiped her eyes and spoke up, full of confidence, while Syr politely nodded, encouraging them to keep going.

"In the western district, she had a stellar reputation. Some male gods even proposed to her. Of course, she turned them down with 'Please don't tease me,' and so on."

"And going out?"

"Hmm?"

"Did she go out much?"

"Well...At the flower shop she worked at, Anna spent a good bit out and about delivering things."

Karen responded, clearly confused by Lyu's line of questioning.

A good disposition. Attractive. Charming enough to catch a god's eye at a glance. And her job involved traveling through the city enough to be noticed. After hearing that, Lyu's confidence increased. *Most likely, they were after the girl from the beginning.*

"...A girl that cute would have definitely been sold to the Pleasure Quarter. Argh! Who knows what is happening to her now!"

"Have you tried asking the Guild or *Ganesha Familia* for help?"

"It's hopeless. The city is overflowing with similar reports. This happens every day. No one will be able to respond immediately."

Karen shook her head as she shot down Syr's suggestion to seek help from the Guild—the city's highest administrative authority—or a well-known familia that worked closely with them to police Orario.

Even if they tried to request an unofficial quest, it could only end in heartbreak because they did not have nearly enough money for a suitable reward.

"If only *Astrea Familia* were around..."

Lyu struggled to rein in her feelings so they would not show on her face as Karen absently whispered her plea.

"Just stop it already! Talking about a familia that doesn't exist anymore..."

"But if Goddess Astrea were around, I know she would help people like us! Why would such a kind familia just disappear...?"

After she finished speaking, Karen clutched her chest and broke down into tears. Huey's gaze shifted into the distance as he went silent.

Astrea Familia. The faction of the goddess whose emblem was the winged sword of justice. During the Dark Age when the Evils ran free in the city, they worked to maintain Orario's law and order, fighting the strong and protecting the weak. This familia of justice no longer existed.

The familia that Lyu used to belong to.

"..."

Lyu stayed silent as Karen sobbed. Syr, Ahnya, and the rest who knew Lyu's past studied their elf coworker with mixed expressions.

Busily working at the middle of the counter was Mia, who had yet to bat an eye at the story. She pretended not to hear the conversation, as if she didn't want to know how things shook out.

Lyu questioned herself as she heard their sad voices.

I quit already. No more helping strangers I've never met without asking for a reward or any compensation. I decided it would only be for the people around me. No more, no less. I can't be the one to bear the standard of justice anymore.

Lyu recalled the conclusion she had reached after falling into a firestorm of vengeance once.

Even though it would only be more hypocrisy...

The smile of a goddess who adored children flashed through her mind, along with images of her comrades in the familia. Above all, she remembered a close friend, a red-haired girl who had argued with Lyu—*If you ever feel lost, stop thinking about complicated stuff! Just be true to yourself!* Her goddess's blessing, still engraved on Lyu's back, suddenly ached.

Lyu closed her sky-blue eyes and sighed at the budding emotions she could not hide in her heart.

That evening, the sky was a dark blue. The moon watched over the giant walls that enclosed the city. Around midnight, Lyu walked along a side street by herself. The Benevolent Mistress was closed, and cleanup had ended. Syr had gone home, and the others split up to go to bed like always. The only one not back in her room yet was Lyu.

She had secretly left the tavern, wearing a long hooded coat and a lengthy skirt. Dressed as though she was selling flowers around the slums, she walked past dwarves and animal people drunkenly snoring by the side of the road. Many shops were closing, but the Shopping District and the Pleasure Quarter were just getting started. Orario didn't sleep, no matter how late. Even on this backstreet, the light of magic-stone lamps leaked out from several taverns out onto the street as they continued serving laborers or adventurers searching for a cheap place to drink. Her hood pulled over her head, Lyu stopped in front of a certain bar nestled in an alleyway where the hustle and bustle of the main street did not reach.

"..."

She descended a set of stairs and opened the beaten-up wooden door.

The scene that greeted her could only be found in a run-down, hole-in-the-wall establishment like the one she just entered. She saw a bony, guffawing chienthrope, a provocatively dressed Amazon who brushed off advances with her smile, and various demi-humans, their deep voices booming, huddled together at wooden tables. A smoky odor wafted in the air, as if something was burning.

A group of men in armor who seemed to be regulars were drinking and accosting every woman who passed by. Whether they were adventurers or not, clearly they were troublemakers. The place was a true den of iniquity.

As all the patrons inspected the new arrival in their midst, Lyu cut through the interior with practiced ease. Attracting suspicious gazes, she stopped in front of a table with a mound of gold coins and cards spread across it, where several men were gambling.

"You're a new face...Something you want from a place like this, Miss Elf?"

The one who spoke was a large human man with a sword at his waist. A grin crept across his face as he examined her attractive features and distinctly elfin ears peeking out of the hood. Demi-human men and women who appeared to be adventurers surrounded him. With subordinates on every side, he was clearly the one in charge.

"Does the name Anna Kreiz mean anything to you?"

As the distressed couple was leaving, Lyu had asked Huey where he had gone to gamble. At first, he had been drinking at a tavern on a major avenue, but after he had accrued losses he couldn't afford, he was taken to a back-alley bar—this one.

"What, you her friend or something?"

The man's grin widened as if he had just found an interesting new plaything. His underlings moved toward the exit, blocking Lyu's way out.

"That girl's a jewel, you know. No one would believe she was just some ordinary city girl, just looking at her. I wanted to give her a go, too, ha-ha-ha!"

"I'd like you to tell me where she is now."

"Oh, I see, I see...And you were expecting that for free, I suppose?"

At this point, everyone in the bar was watching Lyu and laughing or grinning scornfully. Finally, the man hauled himself from his slouch across the chair into a proper sitting position.

"So, missy, know how to play cards?" he asked as he drew a card from the deck on the table. "Since you came here all alone, you must be pretty confident in your strength, right? I'm not fond of brute force, though, so I was thinking maybe we could play a game. I'll bet the information you're after. You can bet money, maybe even put yourself up if you don't have enough to cover the wager."

"..."

"That's how this started, after all. That poor excuse of a father bet his only daughter, played a game, and *wound up handing her over* to us."

The man recognized that Lyu was an adventurer, or at least someone comparably powerful. He was taking precautions while simultaneously trying to draw her onto his home field with gambling. Meeting his gaze, she nodded.

"All right."

Placing a bag full of gold coins on the table, she sat in the chair across from the burly man. A split second later, an uproar broke out around her. The adventurers cheered for the spectacle that was about to begin.

"If I win, you'll tell me everything."

"Ah, no problem, no problem. That's *if* you win, though, missy."

Before long, their table was completely hemmed in by spectators excited to watch the game, but also preventing the gorgeous elf from escaping. Lyu squared off against the thug leader, surrounded by a wall of people.

"What are we going to play?"

"How's poker sound?"

Lyu didn't object as the man started to shuffle. Ordinarily, for the various people in the mortal realm, cards meant a standard deck. It was made of fifty-three cards in four suits with twelve cards each, plus one joker that could be used in place of any card. The suits were swords representing war, fruits meaning fertility, coins signifying wealth, and blessing in the form of chalices. One theory was that they originally dated back to the Ancient Times and had been adapted to games in their current form, while another theory held that the gods who descended to the mortal realm brought the designs with them.

Poker was one of many possible games. After cards were dealt from the deck, it was a contest between players to see who could assemble the best hand.

"What's in the bag, missy?"

"Fifty thousand valis."

The man whistled at her response. He furrowed his brow deeply as he cut and shuffled the cards in an easy, practiced manner.

"You should have said so sooner! If you happen to lose that money and still want to continue gambling…Well, then, like I said before, just wager yourself."

"…"

"I've lost count of the number of elves I've sold to the Pleasure Quarter like you. But please don't misunderstand. I didn't do anything to them until they couldn't pay back what they owed, you know?"

The man licked his lips as his gaze shifted to Lyu's slender neck, crawling across her pale skin.

Vulgar jeers and laughter assaulted Lyu's slender ears. It was intimidation. An attempt to agitate her. The psychological battle had already started. The leader of the toughs laughed as he started doling out cards.

"One thing I should tell you."

"Oh-ho-ho, and what's that?"

As her opponent finished dealing, Lyu's sky-blue eyes narrowed beneath her hood."—I won't tolerate cheating."

As she said that, she drew the shortsword at her waist and, faster than anyone could react, stabbed it down into the table.

The entire bar fell silent after the loud crash. Her opponent's eyes went wide and he started to sweat as the naked blade stood right between two of his fingers, a hairbreadth away from piercing his skin. His arm trembled as the card that he had hidden in the palm of his hand fluttered to the table.

"Next will be your finger."

The man went pale as Lyu retracted the sword after her calm declaration.

"Be careful. I always end up *going too far.*"

With a sharp gaze, she offered one final warning. The people around the table nervously gulped.

Naturally, it was only a bluff. Lyu was neither cruel nor brutal enough to actually commit such violence over a game. However, the results were immediate. The man and his henchmen who had lost their insurance broke into cold sweats. She had thrown them off balance, and they could not read her. All that was left was to amuse herself with a normal game. Holding her cards so that the people around her couldn't see, she matter-of-factly built her hand. Lyu knew that in a gamble, someone who had been shaken once would keep jumping at shadows.

"Full house."

"...?!"

As Lyu laid her hand on the table, her wide-eyed opponent crushed his cards in his fist. She had won nine straight hands. The bar was shrouded in silence by this point. The dozens of chips the man had gambled were now gone, and Lyu had built a mountain of gold coins her winnings.

"You have to be cheating!" he exclaimed as he leaped from his seat.

"How rude. I do not have to stoop to your level to win a game," Lyu dispassionately responded.

She was too straightforward and not very good at bluffs. Some would even say that warnings and intimidation aside, she was incapable of bluffing. Without any other tricks, she just simply played the game in a straightforward manner. She took the cards dealt to her, diligently built the best hand she could, then hid behind an unreadable gaze.

Lyu's expression was frighteningly static. It was rare that someone could read her intentions from her poker face, and she never wavered in the slightest at her opponents' bluffs. By the end, when she spoke the lone word "raise," the thug's face looked as if a knife was at his throat.

Lyu often felt that gambling resembled an adventurer's technique and strategy. And with regard to the latter, Lyu had decades of experience with composing strategy in the heat of battle, so she generally saw through her opponents' bluffs without much trouble. The antics of a lower-class adventurer like the man across from her were no better than those of a toddler.

It was a simple matter once she had outwitted her opponent. Not to mention he had never regained his composure after she caught him trying to cheat once.

"You bastard, who are you?!"

"No one of consequence. I'm just here on a friend's behalf."

She recalled her experience when she was still part of *Astrea Familia*. In those days, it was not unusual for her to conduct undercover investigations at gambling parlors fronting for criminal enterprises. Once, they were trying to crack down on a bookie who was hassling normal citizens; another time it was in order to obtain intelligence about the main branch of an enemy organization. Pretending to be a customer and slipping under the bookie's radar took more than just above-average confidence. Technique and strategy were necessary.

The person who had taught Lyu how to successfully gamble was a colleague in *Astrea Familia*. After that prum girl with a wide grin half beat the method into her, she had put what she learned to good use so many times. Lyu could instinctually see how to obtain victory.

"It's my win. Now talk."

Lyu looked up, remaining in her seat as the leader turned bright red and gritted his teeth. He looked around, flustered, before angrily shouting, "Get her, you assholes!"

As I thought, it comes down to this.

Lyu had wanted to finish things peacefully. She sighed as she readied herself while the underlings started to attack.

One minute later…

In less time than it had taken to finish the poker game, the demi-humans were battered and bruised and splayed across the tavern floor.

"Eek!"

"I know you people were targeting Anna from the beginning. Where is she now? Tell me."

Several tables were upside down. The bodies of henchmen were sticking out of mounds of chairs or the bar. Lyu grabbed the boss by the collar and lifted him with one hand from where he had collapsed to his knees. His bruised face twitched as he flapped his mouth like a floundering fish.

"Th-the Marketplace! That's where we took her!"

"The Marketplace…?"

"Those were the guys who gave us the job! 'We'll pay you well, so snatch the girl without roughing her up and bring her here,' they said."

"You're telling me the client was a company?"

The man kept nodding his head as Lyu raised an eyebrow dubiously. She pressed him for more information about who hired him, but all he did was stick to "I don't know."

When Lyu finally stopped questioning him, the women in the bar had all huddled, teary-eyed, in a corner, trembling in fear. Having gotten all she could, she dropped the man and left the tavern behind. Under cover of night, the elf moved through the town and returned to The Benevolent Mistress—but not before heading to a certain place.

The following day, Lyu was working in her usual waitress uniform when a single customer came to the restaurant and sat at a corner table. The time was late afternoon. This was usually when the balance of customers shifted, leaving few normal guests in the tavern.

Surprised that *she* had already appeared, Lyu walked toward her holding a menu.

"What would you like?"

"One black tea. After that, since I'm alone, I'd also like someone to talk with for a bit."

The beautiful woman with aquamarine hair and glasses carried herself with a refined demeanor.

Asfi Al Andromeda. She was an influential force in Orario who claimed neutrality while wielding an information network with broader reach than anyone else. She was also the leader of *Hermes Familia*.

The detour Lyu had made last night was a visit to the home of Asfi's familia. She had left inside the tightly closed gate a letter containing a written request addressed to Perseus. She had signed it with the name Leon.

Lyu withdrew to the kitchen with the order and quickly returned with a steaming cup.

"I didn't think you would come so quickly. Did you already…?"

"Yes, I investigated the location of this Anna Kreiz you wrote of," Asfi responded, elegantly sipping her tea.

The contents of Lyu's letter were a request for information about Anna Kreiz, specifically the whereabouts of the girl who had been carried off to the Marketplace.

"I owed you. At the end of the day, this is all because Hermes was causing problems." Asfi sighed as she grumbled. "A job is a job, and I don't like owing people. This is just paying back a debt—nothing more, nothing less. Obviously, I don't need a reward, either."

She made her position clear so there would be no misunderstanding: Her motivation was purely business and not a gesture of goodwill.

"Thank you, Andromeda."

"Let's move on."

Asfi shifted her glasses to hide her embarrassment at the sincere thanks even after what she had just said.

"Just as you wrote in your letter, the Marketplace—or rather the corporation—took custody of Anna Kreiz. However, by the time I investigated, she had already been sold."

"To the Pleasure Quarter?"

The Marketplace served as a gateway to the city's distribution network. Various goods passed through here on their way in or out of Orario. The sale of people to the Pleasure Quarter was a closely guarded secret, though it happened with great frequency. The Guild turned a blind eye to these practices.

Lyu's face was strained as Asfi responded in a soft voice.

"It wasn't the Pleasure Quarter. Leon, I don't know what you've stuck your nose into, but it would be better for you not to get involved any further."

"You're beating around the bush, Andromeda. Who bought her?"

Asfi's blue eyes narrowed behind her glasses as Lyu's tone hardened.

"The one who bought Anna Kreiz was from one of the casinos' people."

"!"

Lyu went wide-eyed.

"...A casino in the Shopping District? That's not just any gambling den..."

"Yes. Due to investment from sources outside the city and even beyond the country, it has grown too much. Gambling's the biggest industry in the city after magic-stone items. The Guild has no oversight there, so it's the one place in Orario that the *law can't reach*."

In the past, Orario—often called the Center of the World—was missing just one thing: entertainment. In order to meet to the deities' insistent demands, city authorities welcomed foreign capital and know-how from Mayrustra, the Country of Opera; the Paradise City, Santorio Vega; and other famous countries or cities. Thanks to that, countless entertainment options had been constructed in the Shopping District. Foremost among them were the Theater and the casinos.

Within Orario, where people and goods from all around the world gathered, those facilities ended up growing far beyond the control of the city where they were established. Business was booming, and the entertainment venues were set to overtake the magic-stone-goods industry Orario was so proud of. At this point, the Guild had to tread lightly around them. Consequently, the foreign entities that had originally provided the investment capital had complete oversight. It was fair to say these areas were extraterritorial.

"The casino I'm talking about has cooperation from the Guild, and it has contracted *Ganesha Familia* for security."

"..."

"Infiltration is not feasible. And even if that could be done, you would definitely be caught. It's not possible, Leon. Even for you."

This particular casino was where upper-class adventurers, gods, and the wealthy visiting from outside the city went to spend their money. If anything happened to the richest patrons, the city's prestige and reputation would be affected. Strong adventurers were employed to keep out anyone who wasn't properly authorized. *Ganesha Familia* boasted many first-tier adventurers and was one of the preeminent factions in Orario. For a Level 4, second-tier adventurer like Lyu, it would be difficult to evade their guards, and on the off chance it came down to a fight, it would not end easily.

Exchanging glances with Asfi, Lyu was silent for a short while.

"Before anything else, consider that if a scandal occurs, it might even become a diplomatic problem. Orario can act as cocksure as it wants, but...well, at that point you can just call it the Guild's problem..."

"There are branch casinos from several countries in the Shopping District. Which one bought her?"

"El Dorado Resort—the largest one in Santorio Vega. It's known as the Paradise City's Grand Casino."

Lyu's face finally scrunched into a scowl. El Dorado Resort was Orario's most powerful casino.

"The one who bought Anna Kreiz was the owner, a dwarf named Terry Cervantes. It appears he was the one pulling the strings behind the Corporation as well as the street toughs."

In other words, he was the one who first saw Anna and worked behind the scenes to avoid suspicion.

"El Dorado Resort…Terry Cervantes." Lyu whispered the two names.

"A piece of advice, Leon. It's in your best interests not to get involved."

Ending the conversation, Asfi left her payment on the table and exited the restaurant. Lyu remained seated, silently watching Asfi walk away.

"…Hey, Ahnya, do you know what Lyu talked about with her?"

"…Myeah…I heard something or another about a casino, meow?"

Syr watched Lyu from the kitchen entrance. She was washing plates with Ahnya, whose cat ears were quivering. Looked slightly up toward the ceiling, Syr murmured.

"A casino, hmm…?"

Two days later, Lyu was lost.

Her thoughts kept going in circles as she carried out her duties in the restaurant. But it wasn't because she was hesitant about breaking into the casino.

I could force my way in the back of the building from the Pleasure Quarter side…No, that won't work. I heard the security has been strengthened after another familia tried to break in. Digging up from below isn't realistic, either…

In fact, it was the opposite. Lyu was completely committed to helping this total stranger. To fund her campaign, she traded the magic stones and drop items she had been saving to an intermediary, and she had made good progress in gathering the needed equipment. She hadn't thought at all about what would happen after the breakout.

"Stop thinking about complicated stuff." Lyu was being true to her old friend's advice.

The only thing that troubled her was the question of where to break into the casino.

In the evening after sunset, she was going through countless scenarios in her mind as she carried the buckets piled high with trash to the alley behind the tavern.

"...?"

The sound of people talking around the corner in the alley beside the tavern reached her. Surprised that she recognized one of the voices, Lyu peeked around the corner.

"Then I'll take this..."

"Yes, thank you very much."

She saw Syr bowing her head, thanking someone. The other person had finished their part in the conversation and taken their leave, just far away enough that it was difficult to make out their form in the dim light. All Lyu could see was a slender tail at the edge of her vision—probably a catperson's.

"Syr?"

"Oh, Lyu!"

"What are you doing here?"

"Lyu, look at this!"

Dodging the question, Syr excitedly held up a sheet of paper for her to see. It was a letter with a gaudy gold leaf on a white background. It looked like an invitation to a ball.

"Syr, what is that?"

"An invitation from a casino! Someone gave it to me!"

The ever-calm Lyu couldn't help showing her shock for a moment.

"What?!...What do you mean, Syr?"

"I happened to hear your conversation the other day. I thought it would probably be hopeless, but I tried asking an acquaintance if it's possible to get in. And then..."

"...Unbelievable."

"Ha-ha-ha. But if you have this, you can go to the casino, right?"

Certainly, if Lyu had an invitation letter with a pass, then she would be able to enter the Grand Casino normally from the front without breaking in. Lyu kept glancing back and forth between the letter and a smiling Syr.

"It seems that if you aren't rich, you can't get in...My acquaintance said 'pretend to be the person to whom this was addressed.' It's a count from some small country, apparently."

"...Was the animal person earlier the one who arranged this? Was it a man...?"

"Eh-heh-heh. Working at this tavern, you just end up making some friends..."

The invitation was originally supposed to have gone to a VIP in another country. When Lyu tried to probe further about who brought it, though, Syr just smiled and evaded the question.

Just how big is this girl's fan club?

The mystery surrounding Syr deepened again. Lyu knew she was well connected, often receiving stellar reviews from male deities who loved her unpretentious quality ever since she started working as the tavern's greeter.

"Anyway...is it okay if I go with you, Lyu?"

"Wha...?!"

"I've always wanted to see what it was like at a casino, just once~~!"

At that last bombshell, Lyu's finally raised her voice.

"Wait a minute, Syr. Even if you really want to go, that's just...!"

"But look, the invitation says 'for the count and his wife, the countess' right there. If only one person goes, it'll look suspicious."

"..."

Syr held the page up and pointed out where the recipients' names were spelled out. Lyu took a deep breath, unable to argue. She recalled what Chloe and Ahnya had said before.

"She seems normeowl, but that's a lie. Syr is a witch, meow."

Lyu was forced to agree. Syr was supposedly just some ordinary city girl, but she was already two steps ahead.

"Very well. I can't choose my methods, so I'll be counting on you."

"Yep!"

"However, don't leave my side, no matter what. This is going to be a dangerous job."

"Yes, ma'am!"

She felt sick again after hearing Syr's delighted response. Giving the cheerful girl a sidelong glance, she started to modify her plan before noticing there was a word in Syr's explanation that she had overlooked.

"Wait a minute! Syr, you said 'and his wife.' You don't mean…?"

Syr merely smiled sweetly as Lyu looked agitated for once.

The sun had set behind a distant mountain range while night unfurled from the eastern sky. In the blink of an eye, Orario was swathed in twilight. Viewed from above, no one could be blamed for mistaking the Labyrinth City for a sea of stars. Lit by countless magic-stone lamps, the city put on the mask it wore at night.

Tavern girls stood in front of their respective shops calling for customers while street corners overflowed with the sounds of bards singing and playing their strings or woodwinds. The smell of grilled meat mixed with smoke wafting from pubs. Adventurers returning from the Dungeon and laborers finished with work mingled along the main street, drinking and making merry to bring their days to a close. On top of everything, excitable deities who loved their children were out and about as well. The night in Orario was just getting started.

In the midst of that, the city wall's South Gate opened. A long column of carriages and attendants proceeded along South Main Street from outside.

The richly decorated carriages that passed the inspection point and entered the city were shockingly lavish, and the demi-humans who stepped out of them wore elegant clothes. The visitors dispersed to the hotels, the theaters, various high-class bars, and elsewhere in the Shopping District, each and every one of them scions of foreign wealth.

Once a week, Orario would open the South Gate to let in the wealthy from around the world. This was the current Guild leader's one and only political policy: invite wealthy people from outside the city, allow them to mill around as they spent their money, then reap the economic benefits. Of course, there was a strict security check in addition to the visa required to enter the city. Following that, carriages continued into Orario one after the other, carrying merchants, aristocrats, or people with wealth and status.

Inside the checkpoint, one carriage merged onto the main street from a back alley, becoming just another part of the long procession. The carriage pretended to come from outside the gate, looking exactly the same as the rest while waiting its turn to move along until it finally stopped at one corner in the Shopping District.

After opening the door, an elf in a tuxedo stepped down, his light green hair neatly styled in dignified fashion. A large eye patch covered his left eye and half of his face, evoking the image of a certain deity of forging. Even in the middle of the Shopping District where various aristocrats wandered, he stood out, exuding a mysterious allure. The ladies were rapt as the handsome man—or rather the elf woman wearing men's clothes—took the hand reaching out from the carriage.

"Hee-hee, thank you, dear."

"Please stop teasing me, Syr."

"But if we don't act like a real husband and wife, other people might catch on, right?"

Dressed in an evening gown, she took Lyu's hand and stepped down. Syr smiled as if she were enjoying herself, not at all shy about playing the part of the young bride for the night. On the other hand, Lyu regretted going along with the plan to pose as the count and countess.

"More importantly, isn't that dress a bit too bold?"

"You think? I asked a merchant for a favor and had it prepared in secret, but…"

The price for Syr's long evening gown, combined with Lyu's tuxedo, had set the two of them back quite a bit in rental fees. Needless to say, her outfit was especially revealing. Her slender shoulders and back were bare, plus her chest was barely covered. Normally her cleavage did not appear so large, but in that dress, everything was very prominently displayed. Syr did not seem to mind everyone looking at her, but Lyu was concerned by the lewd stares. Syr giggled when the men scattered in an instant under Lyu's sharp glare.

"As someone who works at a restaurant, I never would have thought I'd get the chance to wear something so fancy."

The long, slender stole hanging between her elbows swayed in the breeze.

Syr had traded her normal hairstyle for one more befitting an evening party, swapping her waitress's white headpiece with an expensive hair ornament. But the person underneath all the accessories was key. With just a little bit of makeup, anyone who didn't know better would easily mistake this girl next door for a noblewoman. Syr was too busy enjoying the attention to realize how alluring she appeared.

*If I don't protect her...*Lyu momentarily seemed like a knight, earnestly bracing herself mentally for the task she had set for herself.

"Look at this, Lyu! He also prepared this fan for me!"

"Don't forget what we are here to do, please."

Syr had taken out a vibrant purple fan and seemed to be playing around, and Lyu tried to remind her of their mission. The local girl stuck her tongue out right before apologizing. Bemoaning her fate, Lyu took Syr's arm, then started walking. The entrance to their goal was a massive arched gateway built to face Main Street.

"Let's see...Today, you are Count Ariud Maximilian, and I'm Countess Sirène Maximilian, his wife."

"Maximilian..."

Lyu repeated the name in a daze beside Syr as their surroundings became even livelier with so many people around. There were extravagantly dressed visitors strutting around in their jewels and furs while many sturdy-looking animal people and dwarf bodyguards could be seen. From the South Gate to Central Park, located in the center of the city, Guild workers and *Ganesha Familia* members were placed around every major establishment along South Main Street.

That's Shakti...So she's here, too. Lyu had been casually looking around when she noticed a familiar beautiful woman with azure hair who was *Ganesha Familia*'s leader. Finally, Lyu and Syr arrived at the arch.

"Could you please show me your letter?"

"Of course. This will do, I'm sure?"

Syr showed the invitation to the human in uniform at the gate. The man glanced over the papers, then greeted them both with a smile.

"It is a pleasure to welcome you, Lord Maximilian. Please have a wonderful evening."

They walked past the employee, as well as the formation of *Ganesha Familia* members facing outward, as they crossed the threshold of the arch. Inside the large plaza, there was a giant fountain surrounded by a group of ornate buildings that were highlighted by multicolored magic-stone lamps.

Far removed from the day to day, this was a gambler's paradise.

Lyu and Syr headed into the resplendent casino.

3

In the south of Orario, the Casino Strip of the Shopping District was filled with places to gamble. The various venues established by several foreign countries and cities also had hotels attached to them. Many buildings had been designed to emulate the aesthetics of different cultures and climes. For example, there was one that resembled an oasis in a desert. Buildings more than three stories tall towered over the elliptical plaza on every side. Yashi trees from the south were growing here and there. In the center, a breathtakingly giant fountain launched sprays of water into the air almost like a giant wave at sea.

The moment Lyu and Syr passed through the giant arch to enter the Casino Strip, a flood of light greeted them. The highest quality magic stones the city had to offer sparkled in red, blue, purple, and gold, illuminating the casinos in the darkness. Unlike Guild Headquarters at the Pantheon or Babel, even the exteriors were vibrantly glowing. Viewed from the sky, there was no mistaking it. As twilight settled on the Labyrinth City, the Casino Strip was the brightest spot for miles around, shining like a sparkling, nightless castle protected by countless guards. This was a different world, set apart from the normal districts of Orario crowded with adventurers and regular citizens.

"There's a lot of people, isn't there?"

"Yes, all of them are extremely wealthy patrons hailing from outside the city."

Syr and Lyu walked through the Casino Strip.

After explaining the situation to Mia, the pair had just barely managed to secure a day off. And now they were slipping into a crowd of privileged elite who were strutting around as if they owned the place. Wearing an expensive tuxedo and evening gown, respectively, they linked arms under the pretense that they were a foreign noble couple.

Deep down, Lyu could not completely suppress her surprise and slight embarrassment as Syr clung to her arm. She was going to have trouble keeping up this masquerade all night. It was difficult to tell whether the platinum-haired girl realized what she was doing, but her shoulders seemed to be quivering in amusement.

"So where is Anna?"

"The El Dorado Resort. That building over there."

Whispering, they faced a building that stood out even in this plaza. Its sumptuous, gorgeous, shining facade could trick one into thinking it was a massive mound of gold. It seemed to have a magical ability to raise the spirits of anyone who looked at it. Statues of deities who symbolized wealth or success were installed around the entrance, either as a perfunctory show of respect or to share in their favor and blessings. A billboard lit up by magic-stone lamps displayed the words THE GOLDEN CITY in Koine, the universal language.

El Dorado Resort. Financed and established by the Paradise City, Santorio Vega, this was Orario's number one gambling establishment, the Grand Casino.

It was also run by the man who had stolen Karen and Huey Kreiz's daughter, Anna.

"Wooow, amazing!"

Passing through the foyer, they were greeted by employees of El Dorado Resort and stepped out into an enormous hall. Syr's cheeks flushed with excitement at the spectacle unfolding before her eyes. The first thing that came into view was a breathtakingly large magic stone chandelier, followed quickly by the luxuriously vibrant and elaborately patterned carpet as well as the variety of tables where people were playing all kinds of attention-grabbing games.

Cards glided from dealers' hands as though they moved along a flowing river. Colorful dice danced through the air while roulette wheels spun madly, their balls bouncing wildly around. Employees in stylish uniforms and guests in dazzling outfits alike gathered around each table like butterflies flocking to flowers. At every game, stacks of chips were being built, wagered, and paid back out. Around the tables, sighs of despair mixed with thunderous cheers, combining into a never-ending din. The casino was in full swing.

"You've been to places like this before, right, Lyu?"

"I've slipped into gambling halls countless times, yes...but it is my first time in one so large."

The pair looked around, passing countless wealthy demi-humans in the narrow space as they moved through the hall. Guests walking around with armfuls of chips were trying their hand at all of the various games. Just one of the chips they were betting equaled a full day's pay for a normal laborer in Orario, but the players could lose that in a single wager.

It was a scene that would make someone with financial struggles feel faint. Obscene amounts of money were being thrown around like nothing. Expediting the free flow of money in the form of enormous bets was the casino's raison d'être as well as the source of its enormous profits.

In order to cater to the tastes of various races, there were many special games that used crystals and jewels, spinning tops, or other tools instead of cards. The elves sampling a different culture and the dwarves cutting loose fit in right alongside the deities. One god tried to casually pocket a handful of someone else's chips, but vigilant *Ganesha Familia* guards stopped the culprit before leading him off to a back room somewhere with a smile. With the help of Orario's adventurers, the establishment's antifraud measures were out in full force.

The dealers at each table added their own flair to the games. A delightful symphony unfolded as they seamlessly shuffled and dealt cards, instantly split chips before sliding them across the table, or rolled dice made of rare crystal only found in the Dungeon. The skillful performance was merely one of many techniques the casino workers used to mesmerize the guests. The dealers were predominantly women, and all were beautiful. They watched with a smile as the guests swung between the extremes of joy and sorrow.

A wealthy prum groaned as his mountain of chips was taken away, while the booming laughter of an Amazon who had just won big rang out from another corner.

"Do you think it would be okay to take one of those chips home? Chloe and the rest really, really wanted to come to the casino, so that could be a nice souvenir..."

"Syr...if you brought that back, I think they would be even sadder at the waste of money."

Syr seemed to be enjoying the vibrant atmosphere in the casino, but her constant wide-eyed staring did not fit her aristocratic appearance in the formal evening gown. Unlike her, Lyu was stealthily glancing around the hall while carefully maintaining the composure befitting a count. She noted the layout of the building as well as the number and position of guards around the room.

"By the way, Lyu...Getting inside is good and all, but what should we do now?" Syr whispered as they walked along the full-floor luxurious rug.

"First, we need to draw attention," Lyu responded simply.

"?"

"We'll make a show of being wealthy. Once people think 'this might be a good customer,' they'll come to us on their own before long."

Lyu's confidence came from the experience she had gained during her time with *Astrea Familia*. Casinos were always looking for potential regulars. A guest who consistently bet piles of money whether they were winning or losing was assuredly wealthy. When management noticed, they would welcome the guest personally—and most likely ask, "Would you like to play a higher-stakes game?"

"I looked at the letter, and this was the first time the count and countess have received an invitation. Being rural aristocrats is convenient for us. Taken another way, it means the casino doesn't have much information about us. We have the advantage."

If a rural aristocrat had more money than expected and spent more money than predicted, that would be a pleasant surprise for the casino. It was their best chance at infiltration. They would pretend to be first-timers enjoying themselves at the casino until management came to welcome them wholeheartedly—unsuspectingly inviting the pair into their inner circle.

"So in other words…just spend a lot of money and get noticed?"

"Yes. But needless to say, the funds we have are limited. It would be best to simply keep winning."

By amassing a large enough number of chips, they could wow the people around them, becoming a focal point of envy and attention. If they then exchanged those chips for expensive drinks, food, and services, management would not be able to ignore it. Even if they were spending chips that had been won at the casino instead of hard currency, customers with open purses were crucial.

Our current goal is to get inside that door.

Lyu had already made a mental note. At the back of the main hall, past countless tables, was a dignified set of firmly shut oaken doors. Only special guests could enter. Two sturdy guards stood on either side of the door, like gatekeepers.

The VIP room. Every casino had one. A place set aside solely for high-stakes games and gamblers who were very free with their bets.

"That reminds me, how much money do you have, Lyu? I brought as much as I could, but…"

"About one million valis. It's pocket change compared to everyone else here. If I had more, this would be a lot simpler…"

Combining her savings with what she had gathered by selling off her tools and items during breaks at work, one million valis was the most she could collect for her war chest. If they could not grow that into a significantly greater amount, that would be the end. For a normal person like Syr, getting rich in one night was just a dream, even at a gambling paradise. But Lyu would not find it much easier, despite the training and experience she had to her name. Either way, they just had to try. In the worst case, there was still the option of a more violent extraction, but she would try the simpler way first. She headed toward one of the tables to exchange her money for chips.

"Ooo, you won again! You're on fire today, Guild Chief!"

"Gah-ha-ha-ha! What do you mean? The goddess of luck always grants me her blessing! That's because I work myself to the bone day and night for the sake of Orario!"

On their way to exchange chips, they heard a loud laugh from one corner of the hall.

"Ah, that elf—I've seen him before."

"Royman Mardeel. Current head of the Guild."

Lyu unconsciously furrowed her eyebrows at the man's vulgar, roaring laughter and pitifully obese torso.

Royman Mardeel. He was effectively the most powerful person in the Guild. Corrupt, rotund, oozing money and power—he was the exact opposite of the typical elf, a race famous for their physical beauty. Royman was loathed by the other elves living in Orario, earning him the moniker "the Guild's Pig." The rumors that he wallowed in debauchery in the Shopping District for days at a time appeared to be true. Even if he was just another influential person relaxing at the end of the day, it was hard for Lyu to watch a fellow elf behave like him. She gave him a sidelong glance as his belly wobbled with laughter before heading in the other direction.

"There could be other people like the head of the Guild who might recognize us. Since normal people can't get into the casino, we need to be careful so that we aren't recog—"

While they walked, Lyu was urging Syr to be careful when a loud voice cut her off.

* * *

"Wait! Please wait!! I've had enough, so please let me go!"

They heard a pitiful young man's voice.

"""..............."""

Lyu and Syr quietly looked at each other as they heard a voice that was extremely familiar. They both slowly turned their heads. They immediately noticed a white-haired human. He was wearing a hastily prepared formal suit that was a couple levels below Lyu's. Hair as white as virgin snow flopped to and fro like rabbit ears. On the verge of tears, he was the very image of a scared little child. Seeing the boy's face appear in the crowd, they exchanged glances again and nodded. Turning around, they maneuvered themselves behind him as he pleaded with someone.

"Like I said, I haven't finished moving in yet! And if my goddess or the others find out, I…I…!"

"…Mr. Cranell."

The boy, Bell Cranell, was startled as he suddenly heard Lyu's voice behind him. His shoulders trembled violently as he turned slowly, half-frozen. His rubellite eyes went wide as he recognized Lyu and Syr.

"L-Miss Ly—gmph?!"

"Refrain from doing anything that could give away our identities."

Lyu quickly put her hand over his mouth as he started to raise his voice.

Bell looked confused for a moment at her warning before suddenly turning red, then nodding like his life depended on it. Removing her fingers from his lips, Lyu took a step back.

"Umm, Miss Lyu, right? And Miss Syr, too…"

"Good evening, Bell. What a coincidence that we meet in such a place. You really surprised me there."

"Mr. Cranell, why are you here?"

"I…well…um, how do I explain it…"

Before the thoroughly confused boy could grasp the situation or give an answer, a deep voice interrupted from behind him.

"Hey, Little Rookie, what are you doing? Our talk ain't over yet."

"M-Mord…"

Following Bell's gaze, they saw a human man with a rough-looking face who was clearly an adventurer. A pair of humans accompanied him. Both Lyu and Syr recognized him as the adventurer named Mord. He had picked a fight in The Benevolent Mistress once and gotten thrown out. On another occasion, he had set a trap for Bell on the Dungeon's eighteenth floor. His ratty, poorly fitting tunic and open collar were hopelessly out of place in this setting. With an appearance like that, the nobles and wealthy patrons in the hall would only see a disreputable person from the moment they laid eyes on him. Given he was an adventurer, this was no surprise.

The other two men who approached appeared to be his friends.

"Don't talk about leaving after all the work we did to convince the casino staff to let you come in with us!"

"No, but I…I still haven't finished moving in yet…! And I don't have any money! And the deposit on these clothes…"

"Don't worry, it's my treat! Thanks to you, I won a ton betting on the War Game! Ha-ha-ha, I'm paying you back, so just accept it like a man!"

So that's what's going on.

Lyu could guess Bell's situation as she watched Mord wrap his arm around the struggling boy's shoulder. He probably had run into Mord by chance and been dragged here. Someone as timid as Bell would have had trouble turning him down. Or maybe he had been brought here on false pretenses.

She wondered what had changed Mord's heart so much that he was laughing and wrapping his arm around Bell, when he was the one who performed an adventurer's "baptism" on the boy in the past. Lyu looked on with a gaze that seemed to disapprove of the delinquent adventurers dragging Bell into the city's nightlife.

"Can I help you, Mr. Aristocrat? If you've got a problem, instead of staring at me like that…Huh?…You seem familiar…"

"M-Mord!"

"Wasn't she at that bar?!"

"Geh! That Bene—"

"Stop talking."

""""—Gah!""""

Lyu had kicked Mord's and his friends' shins so fast none of the guests around them even noticed, ensuring they did not give away her true identity.

"Sorry, I overdid it."

""""Guaaaaaaaa!""""

"Augh...don't be so quick to start a fight, Lyu!"

Syr scolded her as the three adventurers hunched over in pain after being on the receiving end of a low kick from a Level 4. Lyu started to look uneasy as their moaning drew attention. Bell started to sweat.

"Anyway, why are you two here? And why are you wearing an eye patch...?"

"In order to infiltrate the casino, I am pretending to be a certain count. It wouldn't have been possible to get in otherwise."

"I see, and that's the reason for the gown...Miss Syr is wearing..."

Ignoring Mord and company, who were busy groaning in pain, Bell peppered Lyu with questions. His voice tapered off as his gaze shifted to Syr. Her slender shoulders and white back were bare. A deep valley between her barely concealed breasts was also showing. His rubellite eyes were transfixed by Syr's beautiful figure in the alluring gown.

Noticing Bell's gaze as he instantly turned red, Syr blushed. She smiled with a mixture of happiness and devilish amusement, quietly covering her chest with both hands.

"Eh-heh-heh, Bell, are you enchanted by my dress?"

"Uh...umm...sorry!"

As he apologized, face shifting into an even brighter shade, Lyu moved a hairbreadth behind his back.

"*Mr. Cranell.* Refrain from staring at Syr with such ill-mannered eyes."

Lyu's sky-blue eyes narrowed sharply, and her tone was chilling. Recognizing the murderous intent dripping from her warning, Bell apologized for his transgressions, looking like he had seen a ghost.

© NIRITSU

"I-I-I-I'm sorry!"

The elf stared at him for a while as tears welled up in his eyes, before she finally sighed. She should not have been so bothered that he had gone head over heels for Syr, but for some reason she couldn't let it go.

Why can't I overlook it?

Pondering if it was due to the elf value of propriety, she eventually decided the reason was that his gaze had been too lascivious when he looked at Syr.

"Anyway, Mr. Adventurer, why are you all here? I've heard this is the biggest casino in Orario, but..."

"Ho-ho-ho...That's a good question, miss."

Feigning curiosity, Syr turned to Mord's group. The three men who had been groaning rose to their feet unsteadily and started to smile.

"Because we have this here Gold Card! It's a pass only given out to guys who drop a ton of money in the Casino Strip, and it's good for entry at every establishment here!"

With excessive pride, Mord held up a garishly sparkling gold-colored metal card.

"Unlike the other places on the strip, El Dorado Resort is the Grand Casino. And today we were finally able to get in!"

"From Bronze to Silver...and finally Gold. It was a long road to get here. Do you know how much money we had to spend in order to be acknowledged here?"

"We're probably the only third-tier adventurers to have this baby!"

The three friends became teary-eyed as they spoke. Standing between Scott and Guile, Mord appeared especially proud.

In other words, the casino had "recognized" them. As Lyu had explained to Syr earlier, they were considered valuable customers because the trio had burned through so much of their own money. They had been granted the privilege to freely use the casino, and so management had issued them a special pass. Bell had been able to enter on the introduction of the Gold Card holder Mord, though it would have been out of the question for a stray adventurer like Lyu, who was on the black list.

Or perhaps it was more likely that Mord and his friends paid their way in as promising new adventurers after the results of the War Game the other day.

"It's a special privilege available to Orario adventurers—not only the upper-class adventurers! If you spend enough money, you can gain recognition and special services. As long as we mind our manners, even guys like us can get into the Grand Casino."

Certainly, an upper-class adventurer who could bring back valuable magic stones and drop items from beyond the middle levels was more dependable than a rich person with no skills. Even more so if they were a member of a powerful familia. However, the adventurers and factions that could afford to mindlessly flaun6 that kind of money would normally be limited to those in the first- and second-tier adventurers categories. If a third-tier adventurer like Mord was here, he must have spent an unimaginable amount of money, using up everything he recovered from the Dungeon day after day.

"...I am beginning to understand why you all are still only third-tier."

""""Sh-shut up!""""

Their passion withered a bit under Lyu's stare. *However, this is convenient.* Looking toward the oak door, she whispered to Mord.

"I want to know about the VIP room beyond that door. Know anything?"

"Huh? You want to get in there? That's hopeless..." Mord shrugged as Lyu tried to probe his experiences at the casino for information.

"Look at the two guys standing in front of the door—they ain't *Ganesha Familia.* Same goes inside there, too. Even *Ganesha Familia* can't go near the VIP room, let alone get in. That's controlled by casino management. That's where you'll find the real extralegal territory."

"So anyone who can't be trusted to keep quiet about what goes on inside won't be allowed in?"

"Yeah. According to one drunken VIP I ran into, the rumors that they enjoy themselves with high-stakes games are true...and that after, the owner's mistresses come out. The guy's a pervert who surrounds himself with crazy-hot women. Likes to flaunt them in front of the VIPs. Tch, always going on about adventurers," Mord spat back.

Lyu's confidence increased as she listened to his explanation. If she was going to meet the owner who had purchased Anna, as well as Anna herself, it would be behind that door.

"Also…there are stories that new members going back there get 'baptized,' you know? They say he eats them alive. It's only whispers, but…well, like I said, the owner is a giant pervert…You know what I mean, right…?"

I don't know why you came here, but it's better to not stick your neck out—Mord was trying to warn her.

"…I see." Lyu's reply came in a low voice, ending the conversation.

"Uh…umm…I guess I should leave now…?"

"Since you already came to the casino, why not play some, Bell?"

"B-but, if I just play by myself, that wouldn't be fair to the goddess and the others…"

While Lyu was talking to Mord, Syr was beside them inviting Bell to gamble, though his face betrayed his guilty conscience.

"If it's only a little, then I know your goddess, Lilly, and the others won't be mad. And you might not get another chance like this."

"Exactly, Little Rookie, give it a shot. You're a full-fledged, upper-class adventurer now; there'll come a time when you'll regret not enjoying the nightlife. If nothing else, do it for the experience."

Bell struggled to find some reason to run away as Syr and Mord's friends were all urging him to play.

"Um, I don't have any money, though…"

"I'll lend you some. You can pay me back if you win, and if you lose, I don't mind."

"But, um, I don't know how to play cards…"

"How about roulette, then? That's famous enough that even *I* know it. All you do is put the chips down on the table, so it's nice and simple, you know?"

"…Okay, I get it. Then just a little…"

In the end, his resistance was worn down. Rubbing his cheek, Bell resigned himself as he took enough gold coins from Syr to exchange for ten chips.

"Perfect, there's no one at that table in the middle there. Let's go!"

As his conversation with Lyu wrapped up, Mord broke in to lead the group over toward a table. A human dressed as a bunny girl was standing in front of the game table. The beautiful dealer greeted them with a smile. A vibrant black-and-red roulette wheel sat in a silver cradle at the table's edge.

As Syr had mentioned, roulette was very well known, often called the queen of the casino. Once the bowl-like wheel started spinning, the dealer would add a ball, and the player would try to predict which pocket on the wheel the ball would land in. The pockets alternated red and black with different numbers on each one. The player placed chips on a grid of cloth to signify where they thought the ball would land, and if they were correct, they won.

"So I just put the money on top of this sheet?"

"Yes. And there is a difference in payout depending on how you bet. If you bet red or black, then you win two times what you bet, all the way up to thirty-six times if you bet on a specific number."

"Th-thirty-six times..."

"Of course, it's because the odds of guessing a specific number correctly are so low."

Lyu straightforwardly explained the game's rules as everyone watched the first-time gambler step up to the table.

"Evens, odds; you can even bet on a column of numbers. There's no limit on each bet, and you can make multiple bets on a single roll. Well, it's less about learning and more about getting used to it. First, just give it a shot."

At Mord's prodding, Bell timidly exchanged the money Syr had lent him for chips from the dealer. He blushed self-consciously as the cute woman smiled at him before he became nervous again. He studied the table carefully, figuring out where to bet. Once he had finished his painstaking consideration, he chose red, meaning half the possible pockets the ball could land in—a bet with the lowest payoff.

"What's that? After all that, you just chose a color!"

"It's fine, isn't it, since it's his first time. Hee-hee, if you win, Bell, you should give me the winnings."

"Just the color?" Hemmed in by Mord and Syr's back-and-forth, Bell let out a strained laugh.

After confirming the three chips placed on the cloth, the dealer spun the roulette wheel with a practiced hand and tossed the ball in. After making sure there were no new bets or adjustments from Bell or the spectators, the dealer announced the end of the betting window. It was just Bell versus the house.

Seemingly fashioned from an ore mined in the Dungeon, the polished red sphere emitted an inexplicable light as it danced across the fast-spinning wheel. The entire group held their collective breath as they watched the ball slide into the 1 pocket with a *thunk*—a red pocket.

"You did it, Bell!"

"I—I won?"

"Yes, good job."

Syr smiled broadly while Lyu praised him without a change in her expression. Bell's shoulders had stiffened up while the wheel was spinning, but he finally broke into a smile when the dealer pushed his doubled stack of chips back to him. He now had thirteen chips, including what Syr initially loaned him.

"Great, Little Rookie! Let's keep it rolling!"

"Eh, what?! But I already won once..."

"Dumbass! What are you saying you already won once? Didn't you hear little missy here say to pay her back with the winnings?"

"Don't play something small like red or black, go for a bigger payout! Let's grow that stack of chips."

"O-okay, one column this time, then..."

With the encouragement of Mord and friends, Bell nervously put five chips on the table. Lyu sighed as she watched. The dealer tossed the ball into the wheel once, and Bell managed to win again. The payout was triple the original bet.

"You got it right another time, Bell! That's amazing!"

"Ha-ha…It's just coincidence…"

"Alllllll right! Let's ride the momentum, Little Rookie! Go for a bigger bet this time!"

Bell forced a smile for Syr as he bet again: eight chips on a double street bet, covering six numbers for a payout of six to one.

Hit.

"Ah-ha-ha, it's a fluke, a fluke."

Ten chips, a corner bet on four numbers, payout nine to one.

Hit.

"Huh, another fluke…"

Thirty chips, a street bet on three numbers, payout twelve to one.

Hit.

"A f-fluke…?"

One hundred chips, a split bet on two numbers, payout eighteen to one.

Hit.

"…"

Three hundred higher value chips, straight up on a single number, payout thirty-six to one.

—Hit.

"Whooooooooooooooooooooooooooooooooooooooooooooo!"

Mord and his friends screamed as the mountain of chips Bell had built sparkled under the hall's lights.

As they leaned over the side of the table, Syr and Lyu both looked on in a daze, unable to believe what they had just witnessed. Bell himself was standing with his mouth agape, more shocked than anyone else.

"What? What did you say?!"

"Look at that! The roulette table!"

"Look at that mountain of chips…!"

"Who won that?!"

"Wow, it was that white-haired guy, no mistake. The Little Rookie who was the talk of Orario yesterday!"

"The champion of the war game!"

"Little Bell! Isn't that my adorable little Bell?!"

"How much luck can you have?"

"It's the lucky rabbit!"

It was such a shocking win that attention started pouring in from guests all around. Even deities turned to watch as they heard the clamor from Mord's group and the surrounding crowd. Following Mord's suggestion to bet an enormous stack of chips on a single number—and winning—was a big event.

By this point, even the dealer was smiling as she congratulated the novice gambler on his victory. His face twitching in excitement every bit as much as Mord's, Bell unconsciously patted his back, thinking of *a certain slot* in his Status.

"...!"

Syr and Lyu were not about to let this opportunity go to waste. Before people started to gather, they had Bell pay them back *the winnings* from the mountain of chips he had earned.

"Thank you very much, Bell!"

"I'll return the favor, Mr. Cranell. You can be sure of it."

Carrying an armful of high-value chips, they left the table.

"Can you do it again, Little Rookie? We'll put up the money, so let's do it!" "No way! I'm definitely going to guess wrong!!"

As they started their own game, they heard Mord and his friends greedily shouting at Bell in the background.

Their original concern about funds having been resolved, it was now time to make a killing. With the chips that Bell had unexpectedly won, Lyu tore up table after table.

"Straight flush."

Mostly, she avoided games where the casino had the advantage—where the player faced off directly against the dealer—and instead played poker where she could challenge other guests. Thanks to a naturally high level of concentration, her poker face, and the training she had received from an old friend in the familia, she racked up wins and amassed even more money.

"Raise."

Thanks to Bell, she had plenty of funds for her war. Occasionally, she would lose one hand badly on purpose. Then, like a disinterested elite without any care for money, she would bet even more chips, as if to declare the loss had meant nothing.

Because she was betting so much, the other guests at her table were miserable and started to be overly cautious of her hands, shrinking back from showdowns and folding hands that they could have won. Her eye patch did its job, too, making her look mysterious and intimidating.

"Split."

When she did play against the dealer, she always chose the game with the best odds for the player and took advantage of the dynamic vision of an upper-class adventurer. While reading the movement of the cards, she secretly used card-counting techniques her old friend had drilled into her to make as much money as possible, betting at only the best times. Once she had grasped the flow, she created a positive feedback loop.

"Ahhhh! You're amazing, dear!"

And Syr perfectly played the role of a rural count's wife, her eyes sparkling, clapping her hands in front of her voluminous chest, and from time to time hugging Lyu in excitement.

Syr, you're overdoing it…

Hee-hee, is that so?

Lyu wanted to sigh when she warned her partner with a glance and received a childlike smile in return. By then, Syr nonchalantly ordered a high-class drink with a smile, tactfully displaying her dignity.

"Excuse me, sirs, could you gods spare a moment?"

"Oh, Syr! Why are you here?"

"Please keep my real name a secret. Also, I have a little favor I'd like to ask, if you don't mind listening? I'll be sure to give you a lot of freebies the next time you come to the restaurant."

"Go ahead, go ahead, ask anything you want!"

While not compromising her disguise as the countess to anyone watching, Syr also made use of her true identity. Using her wealth of connections as the restaurant's poster girl, she asked favors from the gods of debauchery who were at the casino to play. Those deities, hooked by her cute smile and the lure of freebies, took her up on her request and spread out across the hall.

"Do you know who that man in that striking eye patch from earlier was?"

"I heard he was the Count of Felnas!"

"Isn't Felnas that small country…?"

"Yes, they were supposed to be having some economic difficulties, I thought…"

"It seems they found a mountain of seiros in a forest within their territory."

"What? I'm so jealous!"

"I heard he completed several projects after that, so he's living it up now!"

"Oh, no wonder!"

"He certainly cuts a splendid figure!"

"Look at that, I think he's winning again!"

"I didn't know someone of his caliber existed in that country."

"Yes, he's so young and dignified. How dreamy."

"And the wife next to him is gorgeous, almost like a white lily next to him…"

"And I heard that his wife is a distant relative of the imperial house!"

"That's amazing!"

The gods who had wandered among the crowds were spreading false information as they pleased and fully enjoying it. What started as plausible lies became more and more embellished as the rumors spread through the casino. All according to plan, the entire hall started watching as Lyu won game after game with towering stacks of chips on the line.

"Excuse me, sir."

Just as she was about to bet even more money, an older human wearing a well-tailored black suit appeared in front of her.

"The owner, Mr. Cervantes, would very much like to meet you."

It's begun, Lyu thought as Syr smiled at her side. She was confident they had taken the bait. Without letting her expression shift, she responded.

"It's an honor for the owner himself to say that about a fledgling like me. Where should we go?"

"Please, this way."

Apparently a manager, the middle-aged human, led them with a courteous manner toward a stout dwarf who was circling the floor, greeting guests.

"Oh! You're Lord Maximilian, aren't you?"

Noticing them, he approached with both arms raised. He matched the typical dwarf body shape; the top of his head didn't even reach Lyu's eyes. His beard was in perfect condition, and his brown hair was slicked back. His high-quality black suit bulged slightly from his thick arms, legs, and broad chest. As expected of a person who engaged in a less than wholesome trade, a bodyguard was visible nearby.

"I am Terry Cervantes, the owner of this casino. Thank you very much for coming tonight from so far away."

"Likewise, thank you very much for inviting us. I am…Ariud Maximilian. And this is my wife, Sirène."

"Thank you for giving my husband and me a chance to have so much fun, Mr. Cervantes."

Once Lyu had finished the introductions using their fake identities, Syr politely thanked him, as befitting a woman of her status. The man who came to greet them was not lacking for charm. At first glance, he had a hard face, but he was adept at encouraging people to let their guard down, speaking without breaking his smile.

However, Lyu had dealt with countless people who wore a similar "mask," so inducing her to lower her guard was impossible. Putting up her own facade, she continued to play the part of an aristocrat.

"I wanted to meet you earlier, but there were so many guests tonight…Allow me to welcome you once again, and please enjoy yourselves."

As the manager who had led them here started to leave his seat,

Terry stuck out his right hand. Lyu looked down at his thick hand before refusing.

"I'm incredibly sorry, I've sworn my love to my wife. I'm not permitted to touch anyone aside from her. I hope you can forgive me."

"It's fine, it's fine. It's understandable since you are a pure elf. Your husband certainly loves you, madam."

"Hee-hee, thank you very much."

Lyu alertly sensed a stiffness hidden behind his words.

He must be a dwarf who doesn't get along well with elves. He's not an inexperienced newcomer to Orario anymore, so I don't think he'll make a scene of it yet.

She also did not overlook the flash of lechery in Terry's gaze as he smiled at Syr.

That expression. As I expected…

Lyu's uncovered right eye narrowed, recognizing that her guess had been correct.

"By the way, Lord Maximilian, I've heard that you've had *considerable luck* today. With that in mind, do you think you'd like to come to the VIP room over there?"

Terry's smile switched from an amiable owner's to that of a salesman. He glanced toward the very doors in the back of the hall that Lyu had set her sights on.

"VIP room, you say…?"

"Ah, don't worry, it's simply a place where guests like you can enjoy even greater stakes. You'll find people of similar wealth there, along with the highest-class service and games that can only be played in that room. Plus, plenty of conversations and connections that can only be had with your peers. May I interest you in something like that?"

As expected, he was naturally inclined to invite a prosperous guest with a large number of chips to spend to the VIP room. Pretending to think about it for a moment, Lyu shifted her gaze to Syr, who matched hers with a smile.

"Dear, I'd really like to give it a try."

"If even my wife says so, then if you don't mind…"

"Ga-ha-ha, it's decided, then!"

With Terry leading them, they moved out, heading to the back of the hall while cutting through the crowds of guests.

"By the way, that impressive eye patch...If you don't mind my asking...did something happen?"

"I don't mind. The truth is, once my wife was attacked by monsters...I managed to save her, and the wound was healed with magic...but the eye the beast's claws took did not return." Lyu shared the story they had rehearsed beforehand.

"I see, a badge of honor, then. You truly are a man among men."

Terry praised Lyu casually while examining her face from the side, as if searching for something.

"...Yes?"

"I've had this nagging feeling that I've met you before somewhere...but I suppose it is merely my mistake. I'm sorry, please don't mind me."

A hint of uneasiness floated across Terry's face, but he immediately wiped it away with a smile as they arrived at the oaken doors that were flanked by stout gatekeepers.

"Please, this way."

The tightly shut doors swung open. Following Terry, Lyu and Syr stepped into the enemy's lair.

4

The clamor of the hall faded to silence as the doors closed. A shadowy room lit by magic-stone lamps greeted them. The room appeared as large as the main hall, but there were drastically fewer tables and people around, creating a uniquely grand atmosphere.

Waiters in black suits and gorgeous women wrapped in magnificent gowns poured alcohol for the customers.

"I thought it would be a bit more lively."

"Yes, it's just like a salon."

Lyu and Syr exchanged whispers as they followed Terry.

The VIP room of the Grand Casino of El Dorado Resort.

Escorted in by the owner, Terry Cervantes, Lyu and Syr examined the wide room.

As expected, none of the noise from the hall made it past the oaken doors.

Faint conversations echoed in the spacious chamber. The tables were clearly high-class mahogany, broad and solidly constructed. The guests surrounding them were also a clear cut above the rich and well-to-do outside in both make and manner. Many of them were playing cards with large stacks of chips in front of them. In addition to the guests, there were also handsome waiters moving with absolute precision as well as gorgeous young women in eye-catching dresses. A great many of the latter.

Lyu's eyes narrowed when she caught sight of them.

"Over here, this table."

Terry led them to a table where several guests were engaged in a card game.

Four people. The demi-humans in the seats are seemingly old acquaintances of Terry's since they started speaking up without reservation.

"Tonight's been fun, as always. Thanks, owner."

"Speaking of, who are these two?"

"Allow me to introduce them. Patronizing our establishment for the first time tonight, Lord Ariud Maximilian. And beside him is his wife, the Lady Sirène."

"A pleasure to meet you, everyone."

"Thanks to the owner's kindness, we were able to come here. Please take care of us."

Greeted by smiles, Lyu and Syr finished their introductions, as a waiter neatly pulled a chair out at the table for Terry. As he sat down, an elf girl appeared, carefully setting a cocktail in front of him. Suppressing her feelings at watching a fellow elf treated like a pretty doll, Lyu turned to Terry and asked,

"Mr. Cervantes, these beautiful people we've been seeing are..."

"The girls are...well, it probably doesn't make the best impression, but they are my mistresses. If I say so myself, I courted them quite passionately, and they did me the honor of responding in earnest."

Even if she had not heard it, Lyu had already been sure of the answer. Terry responded without hiding his pride as he settled into his seat.

"Since so many maidens responded to my love, the Goddess of Beauty would surely scold me for keeping it all to myself. It might be a bit presumptuous, but in order to share the wealth, I have them help out with serving drinks."

He said it in a roundabout way, but these girls were in the same situation as Anna Kreiz. Terry took a liking to them after a glance, and then he did everything in his power to control them.

"The owner's a pervert who surrounds himself with crazy-hot women. Likes to flaunt them in front of the VIPs." In other words, the information Mord heard about the VIP room is correct. These people are a part of Terry's collection.

Each and every one of the girls was beautiful in their bold and erotic dresses—and incredibly doll-like. Against their will, they were here for various absurd reasons. Like Anna, all of them had been brought in through illicit channels, whether from inside or outside the city. Various colors of chokers adorned their necks, as if to show that the girls belonged to him.

This room was a part of Orario that was actually *beyond the law.* Even things like this went unchecked. If there were no one to challenge the arrogant owner, then the guests would also enjoy, praise, or partake of the sweet nectar of his collection.

She must also be here...

Tamping down her righteous indignation after seeing the owner's arrogant preening while the guests leered at the beauties around them, Lyu spoke up again.

"Now that you mention it...on the way here, I happened to hear you recently got your hands on a siren-like beauty."

She merely put it out there, but the others at the table quickly chimed in with excitement.

"Ohhh, I had also heard that! Something or another about marrying a woman from some faraway country."

"Do you think you could let us see her?!"

The elites chorused. It was another vomit-inducing picture. Enjoying the attention, Terry grinned.

"Ga-ha-ha! Everyone's ears sure are quick! As you said, I've welcomed a new lover to my fold. Let's have the long-awaited introduction! Hey!"

Whether it was because he felt gratified by their interest, or perhaps he had intended to show her off from the start, the dwarf quickly waved over one young waiter. He bowed respectfully and went through a door at the back of the VIP room to return with a human girl in a pure white dress.

"Pleased to…meet you…My name is Anna."

Lifting the hem of her skirt politely, the girl introduced herself. She could not entirely suppress the fear seeping into her trembling voice. Without a doubt, this girl was the Kreiz daughter.

I see…she is beautiful…

Karen's words hadn't just been maternal pride. Anna was attractive enough that the men of great wealth and particular taste were nodding in appreciation. She had honest blue eyes, white skin, a slender jaw and neck, and a modest bust. From an objective view, hovering on the boundary between a girl and a woman, she was more beautiful than the elf Lyu and was even a rival for goddesses. She had the same choker around her neck as all the other girls.

Her flaxen hair that her mother had boasted about was tied back behind a gaudy hair band, lightly shaking in a way that seemed to reflect her true feelings. She triggered people's protective impulses as her long eyelashes shaded her eyes when she looked downward. The starstruck elites sighed in admiration, lasciviously staring at her bare shoulders.

"This one's also…grade A."

"Yes, splendid. As if a goddess blessed the earth with beauty. Well done finding her."

"The truth is, I stumbled across her while wandering around

foreign lands. It must have been divine guidance. With such beauty and charm, she entranced even me."

As Terry spun his lies, Lyu stared at Anna. Perhaps sensing something different about this gaze among all the inquisitive ones, or possibly perplexed, Anna lifted her head in wonder and locked eyes with Lyu. It was then Terry noticed where her attention was.

"Lord Maximilian, is there something on her face?"

"No…it's only that I know a woman who resembles her."

The air around Lyu changed, as she stepped uncomfortably close to Terry.

"According to my acquaintance's story, he was lured into a gamble by some crooks and dirtied his hands…After having everything stolen, his beloved daughter was taken away from him."

"!"

Both Terry's and Anna's eyes flickered in recognition.

"The girl's father who took the bet was assuredly a fool…However, if you look closely, it appears that the events happened at *a certain person's* instigation."

"…"

"That person set those criminals on the man in order to seize the lovely daughter, and after it was all over, he quietly made the girl his own, it seems…Quite the sad story for those who know her situation."

She had intended to stop herself, but she failed. Lyu realized she was more furious than she had thought. Her words carried a sharp undertone as she turned her gaze toward Terry.

"Even now, I am searching for that girl…chasing down her whereabouts."

Without making it explicit, she made it clear that she knew the entire story and all of the details regarding Anna's situation. The amiable dwarf let his mask slip and glared dangerously at Lyu. A mobster would not have a glare more brutal than his. Only someone who had trod this cruel path could wear such an expression.

Sensing the change in atmosphere, the wealthy guests around the table became flustered, though the more clever ones realized what was happening. The center of the conversation, Anna, was totally dumbfounded. Syr was a noticeable anomaly, visibly unshaken as she maintained her placid smile while watching the proceedings.

Lyu had effectively declared that she had come to take Anna back.

"That's a very interesting story, Lord Maximilian. Incidentally, it's a bit sudden, but I heard that you were the Count of Felnas..."

"Yes, no more than a rural aristocrat. An inflexible, hardheaded elf...one who can't overlook someone on the wrong path."

She met Terry's searching gaze head-on. The guests at the other tables, the waiters, and the mistresses all noticed something strange was happening and shifted their attention toward Lyu and the owner. Silence settled over the VIP room.

"I'm not sure who or where the misunderstanding happened, Lord Maximilian...but it seems you've set aside your wife and become quite passionate about my Anna."

Still staring daggers, Terry finally spoke up, a smile forming above his beard.

"Well then, shall we play a game?"

"Game...?"

"Yes. The person who loses has to fulfill one request made by the winner. It has to be something accessible to the loser, naturally. Also, we'll play the game with the highest-value chips."

He snapped his finger and a waiter emerged pushing a cart holding a tremendous pile of the chips. The mountain of platinum-colored pieces sparkled. The value of all the chips Lyu had collected in the main room could not begin to compare to what was on that cart.

"We'll play with this on loan. It won't be much of a game with any less."

Which means the loser doesn't simply owe a favor, they also take on a large debt, Lyu thought, already caught up in the extortion...*Even so, I have no reason to let him go.*

Other than the man pushing the cart, several more men surrounded the table where Syr and Lyu were seated. Like their colleagues guarding the entrance, they were all muscular.

One...no, two experts are in this group.

Lyu recognized the human and catperson behind Terry in particular as a cut above the rest.

She had not heard anything about a powerful familia being sent out by Santorio Vega. They were probably unaffiliated bodyguards employed directly by Terry—strays who had no familia. They were no match for *Ganesha Familia*'s main branch, but in the VIP room, the owner's henchmen were more than enough to handle any fights that might happen to break out.

"For people like us, who have already achieved wealth, status, and prestige, what we really want…is the thrill of gambling with our lives on the line. Am I wrong?"

As the black-suited bodyguards exerted pressure with their presence, Terry laid out his challenge.

Is he trying to taunt me while setting up a human shield, or is he trying to obfuscate Anna's situation with this game? Well, his proposal is simple.

All you have to do is win. That was all there was to it.

I guess I'll play along for now.

Lyu did not have a special plan that called for letting loose now. Anna was too close to Terry and his bodyguards. And she would be helpless if he called *Ganesha Familia* in from the hall.

Syr is here, too. I should wait and see for now…

Glancing at the girl sitting next to her, Syr gently nodded back toward her.

"…Of course. Let's have that game."

The corners of Terry's mouth turned up in a smile when Lyu accepted his proposition. He looked at the people gathered around the table.

"How about all of you, ladies and gentlemen? This is the Grand Casino! There's no flavor if it is just a one-on-one match between Lord Maximilian and myself! So let's all play with the same conditions: I'll fulfill any request of the winner! Oops, I'll have to decline any dangerous requests like 'I want your life,' though, of course. Ga-ha-ha!"

The flustered guests all looked at each other while Terry spread his arms and made his proposal. Smiles started to spread in the crowd as the owner played up his prestige while mixing in jokes, and in the end a few more guests agreed to the terms. It was practically proof they were hungering for the thrill of standing on the edge between glory and destruction, The preparations were adjusted to include the new players.

"Do you have any preferences for the game? If not, I think we should go with poker."

"I don't mind."

"All right, then the match will be decided by knockout...when all the chips in front of someone are gone, that person has lost."

The dwarf owner's eyes sparkled with amusement as the elf accepted the terms, her sky-blue right eye shining with contained rage. In a flash, the prepared chips were spread across the tabletop. The waiters looked on with frozen expressions, while the mistresses watched with resignation and unease. Anna's gaze wavered as the game began.

"Well then, shall we start with a twenty-chip bet?"

"I'll double that."

The game was flop poker. In addition to the cards in a player's hand, there were communal cards placed faceup in the center of the table that everyone could use. Those shared cards were used to complete the hand. Even with a weak hand, sometimes it was possible to easily win a round by bluffing.

For now, there are no irregularities.

Lyu was obviously watching Terry, but she also focused on the man dealing the cards for signs of cheating. As a former adventurer tempered in the Dungeon, she would not overlook even the smallest abnormality among the other guests. Likewise, the bodyguards were carefully watching her for any sign of trickery—especially the human and catperson at Terry's side.

Other than Terry and Lyu, four other players joined: two humans, one affluent prum, and an elderly gentleman animal person. Without any exclamations, concern, or scene-making, the sound of cards flipping and chips clacking resounded.

Each mound of chips repeatedly grew and shrank. At first glance it seemed like a close contest—

"Oh-ho, this senile old man won, eh?"

"..."

The elderly animal person had won the hand and swept away the chips Lyu had bet.

Even with an upper-class adventurer's tactics of avoiding unnecessary confrontation, the chips she had at hand were running out. She had already lost about half of her starting pile. And it was *only Lyu*. Only she had been unable to win a game. She could not get a read on her opponents. Her strategy wouldn't come together.

Terry sat across from her with the lead in chips, a bold smile creeping across his face. Syr was quietly watching the table next to her as Lyu reflected on what happened.

I was careless...

She shifted her gaze to her surroundings, to the guests. The animal person was sipping high-quality liquor while the affluent prum played with some chips in his hand, a scornful sneer scrawled across his face.

It's not just the dealer. I should have expected the owner and the guests to work together, too.

Their relationship was not merely that of a casino owner and his clients. They were *accomplices*.

She watched them closely and was sure there had been absolutely no tricks. That meant they were using a method that Lyu could not detect to signal the contents of their hands.

Hand signs, exchanging looks, some indication in how they spoke, or perhaps all of the above. They were passing messages in a way only they understood to share information about their cards. Then, when Lyu joined a hand, the person with the strongest hand beat her without fail.

She had to minimize losses and only try when she had a chance to win.

Everyone at this table is against me...

Her opponent was not just Terry; it was all five present in the game.

More than just making a hand using the shared cards, they were effectively sharing their hole cards, too. That was why she could not read into her opponents' thoughts. They had no intention in the least of using any strategy or bluffing. Like a mob of monsters attacking an adventurer, they were trying to break her with the brute strength of numbers.

I didn't notice it, but my anger clouded my vision...

Lyu was forced to admit she rushed in blindly due to her rage. If she were in her normal frame of mind, she would have noticed much faster. However, seeing the terrible treatment Anna was subjected to, on top of the arrogant way Terry and the others objectified the other girls, she had lost her cool and insight.

No, even if I had recognized it when I accepted the bet, it's still likely I would have lost.

She cursed herself for making such an elementary mistake.

"It looks like you've lost quite a lot of your chips. Are you all right over there, Lord Maximilian?"

"..."

She belatedly started to watch her opponents' movements for signals, but that would not be enough to make a connection. As Lyu maintained her silence, Terry spoke up, enjoying himself.

Anna staggered as he pulled her close with his meaty hand. She did not understand the game, but was on the verge of tears after recognizing that the person who had been so mad on her behalf was in a bad spot. Or perhaps it was because she thought Lyu's involvement in the current situation was her fault.

"Now that I think about it, I haven't said what I wanted when I win, have I?"

Snaking his arm around Anna's waist and stomach, the dwarf spoke up.

"In the event I win, I think I'll ask you to let me borrow your partner over there—that lovely wife of yours—for a little while."

Lyu, who had kept a calm composure, finally snapped as he fanned the flames of her rage.

"I'm jealous you were blessed with such a lovely young bride. It's not fair. I want to enjoy a taste, too, I think. A date with drinks over dinner…just the two of us, you know?"

Terry leered at Syr. As she silently glanced back at him, he gave her a vulgar grin.

I see. This is the baptism.

New members brought back to the VIP room, particularly ones who did not conform or tried to oppose Terry, were soon blackmailed into this game. Using the debt they just incurred, they were forced to accept his demands. Even if their intimate partner was what he requested.

New members were eaten alive. What Mord had said earlier finally became clear. With that understanding, an incontrollable fury was born.

"Impertinent people, those blinded by greed…and those moved by a sense of justice like you…I chew them all up and spit everything out."

—Should I start now?

Even if she had been railroaded into it, it went against her pride to abandon a game—a match—halfway through. But that paled in comparison to the irrepressible hatred welling up now.

She could not forgive this man motivated by carnal desire, and his accomplices angling for the chance to share in his profits disgusted her. In response to the elf bristling with deadly resolve, the fence of bodyguards readied themselves. Ignoring her concerns and the risks, Lyu was about to start a brawl.

"Dear."

However, the one next to her reached out her hand and placed it on Lyu's shoulder. Exhaling, she stopped and looked to her side. Syr smiled, as if she had read what Lyu was planning. She took her time shifting her gaze to Terry and the guests.

"Everyone, it seems my husband is a bit tired. That being the case, do you think you could let me play in his stead?"

Even Lyu was shocked at that proposal.

"Syr—"

"Dear, please. I want to decide my fate with my own hand…I don't want to have it be your fault that I have to commit to something. Mr. Cervantes, in the event I lose, then I'll obey your request. So please don't do anything to my husband."

"Bwa-ha-ha-ha-ha-ha…a husband and wife's love is a truly beautiful thing, isn't it? Yes, I promise, madam."

Lyu was unconsciously leaning forward, only held back by Syr's pleading gaze and words. How did this exchange look to everyone else? An admirable young bride's devotion, or perhaps sacrificing herself in order to protect her husband?

However, she knew it was neither. Syr's exaggerated performance as *the countess* brought Lyu back to her senses. Constructing a delicate smile with perfect technique that she used to subdue her colleagues at the tavern, the girl stood up.

"Mr. Cervantes, do you think you could listen to one more request?"

"What's that?"

"I'd like to see the person to whom I owe my life. If you could call him into the room?"

A look of disbelief crossed Lyu's face. *She can't mean…*

"The truth is, the person who saved my husband and myself from danger was *a certain adventurer* who happens to be here tonight…"

"…"

"My husband and I had planned to have dinner together, then grant him a reward tonight. However, in the event I am having drinks with you, I won't be able to do that. So…I wanted to properly say good-bye."

As Syr spun a web of nonsense, Lyu contained her urge to look at her in shock, determined to keep quiet and leave this to her. Terry's eyes narrowed in suspicion as the count and countess put up a brave front—or at least pretending to.

"It's fine, of course. I'll grant special permission for him to enter the VIP room."

"Thank you very much."

After hearing a description of the adventurer, one of the guards left the room.

A short while passed before the white-haired boy was brought in, a look of utter confusion on his face.

"That white hair…without a doubt, it's the Little Rookie."

"Bell Cranell? The one from the War Game the other day?"

As expected, Lyu thought as the other guests whispered.

Confused by the atmosphere of the VIP room, Bell swung his head back and forth without rest, as if he had wandered into a foreign world. Why had he been called out? What was Syr thinking? Lyu had no clue.

However, she trusted Syr.

After all, she was so cunning that her colleagues in the bar called her a witch, and she was able to see two moves ahead of a former adventurer like Lyu; she was even acknowledged by deities. Her true essence was *determination*.

"I'm very sorry, Mr. Cranell. Unfortunately, I have an appointment after this. Please allow me to cancel the meal we had planned."

"Eh…uh…ummm?"

Bell became increasingly confused. He had been brought to the table without a clue of what was happening, and once he finally reached Syr, she greeted him with a reference to a conversation he did not remember having.

Bell looked around the shadowy VIP room: Terry and the other guests laughing derisively, the imposing bodyguards, Lyu surrounded by them at the table, and countless beautiful women in gowns.

His jaw stiffened, and his gaze returned to Syr, who stood in front of him.

"S-Syr?"

"Please call me Sirène here, Mr. Cranell."

As she whispered and shifted a little closer, a playful smirk flashed across her face for a split second.

"M-Miss Sirène…are you…busy with something?"

In response to his question, she smiled and put her finger in front of her lips.

"A no-good game."

"..."

"Is that okay with you, Mr. Cranell? This VIP room is a place that even members of *Ganesha Familia* may not enter...so no one can come in. Even if something happens, no one can come in here, not even someone as gallant as you."

Bell's eyes went wide as Syr seemingly whispered a warning to him. Everyone in the saloon leaned in to hear their conversation, while Lyu intently observed the state of affairs.

Finally, Syr earnestly said, "I was really glad to be able to see you... Let's meet again if chance allows."

"Miss Sir...ène..."

"Finally, would it be okay to shake your hand?"

At her teary-eyed entreaty, he timidly clasped his hand around hers. As if to accept his warmth, Syr grasped his hand tightly.

"Thank you...and farewell."

Rubbing her eyes, she turned away. Bell was led out of the room with bodyguards on either side of him.

"What's this? Your wife is a woman of affairs, isn't she, Lord Maximilian?"

"..."

Lyu did not respond to Terry, who had watched the sorrowful performance from start to finish with a smirk. It was natural her behavior would look like love, since she had indeed given her heart to the boy, though Lyu could not say that.

"Have you finished with your good-byes?"

"Yes."

Returning to the table, Syr nodded in response to Terry as she sat down. Seeing a resolute look on her face after she wiped her eyes, Terry asked, "Then, I think we should start...Incidentally, do you know the rules of poker, madam?"

"Yes, at the shop...I was invited on occasion by some mischievous maids, and I enjoyed myself without telling the master."

As Syr promptly corrected herself, Lyu donned a complicated expression. When she mentioned "people from the shop," she most likely meant Ahnya and Chloe. If they were here, there was no doubt that the pair would object to being turned into maids in her story and loudly complain.

And the master she mentioned was not Lyu, but Mia. It was the tavern staff that had been secretly playing behind the owner's back, and they had invited Syr to join.

"It's a little embarrassing, but I'm not very familiar with the more exotic kinds of poker...Would draw poker be okay with you?"

Draw poker was a game where each player was dealt five cards with which to make a hand, and they were allowed to exchange cards once. Among all the different kinds of poker games, it was the most fundamental. The rules of the original bet and each person's stack of chips would not change, so Syr inherited the shrunken stack that Lyu had left. With no sign of any objections, her request was accepted.

"Also, one more thing."

Clasping her hands together in front of her chest, Syr added one more request.

"Anyone who folds must pay twice the ante. How does that sound?"

Syr smiled, implying it was a rule she learned from the maids with whom she often played. It could be thought of as a forced bet... However, Terry and the other players were confused at the complete reversal from her previous meek behavior.

"Well...that's fine."

Puzzled, they glanced at each other, accepting the request in the end.

Things got a little bit weird, but that didn't matter.

Glancing aside as the dealer dealt the cards, Terry fixed his gaze directly in front of him, across the table.

The player was Syr, while Lyu was standing behind her. Staying constantly vigilant against anyone who might try to peek at the girl's cards, she moved closer like a protective man-at-arms. The mysterious elf with the eye patch glanced at Terry.

You haughty elf bastard...I knew at first sight that I couldn't stomach you. Trying to act the honorable knight, sacrificing himself to save some princess...

Terry shifted his gaze from Lyu to Syr, his sadistic streak instantly rearing its head.

I'll steal your partner and ruin that cute little face of hers.

The countess is a beauty in a different way than Anna. She may have an unsophisticated face and light makeup, but those breasts are surprisingly ripe, plus her arms and legs look luscious. I haven't had a chance to play with Anna yet, so it'll be fun to sample them together.

As rumored, he had performed this baptism in the VIP room countless times. Those foolish enough to oppose him were forced into servitude by the weight of crushing debt while he stole the countless women and items that he had coerced players into wagering as collateral in the game.

Naturally arrogant and disrespectful toward people of wealth and prestige, it would only be natural for Terry to be surrounded by enemies. But instead, he used the carrot and stick to control the people around him. He had no mercy for those who opposed him, while those who pledged allegiance received excellent treatment.

The guests who joined the baptism also profited. They reached out a hand of kindness to the new member grieving in defeat. Having someone powerful enough to be invited to the VIP room owe them a favor was valuable, and having experienced it themselves, they could more convincingly win over the new recruit. This web of profitable relationships increased the lackeys he could call on, solidifying Terry's position as the unassailable absolute authority in the Grand Casino.

Terry believed without a doubt that he was the king of this gambling paradise—perhaps even all of Orario.

The Guild can't interfere with us. And even if someone tries to come at me with force, I have Faust and the others to take care of it.

The human and catman bodyguards were positioned behind him. He had paid a large sum of money to hire men who were strong, and these two had made a name for themselves with their abilities. These warriors would make even upper-class adventurers shudder. When people would not bend no matter how much he threatened and blackmailed, those two would bury them quietly.

More importantly, they would instantly see through any tricks Lyu or Syr might try in this game. With all the other guests working as *accomplices*, Terry's victory was assured.

Bastard, I'll have you groveling at my feet!

Finally, the dealer finished his task and gathered the ante put in by all the players.

As Terry and his four co-conspirators secretly grinned in anticipation, the game began.

—Immediately after that.

"Wow! Look at this, dear!"

Syr called excitedly as her blue-gray updo bounced.

"Look, four of the same card! That's four of a kind!"

Terry, the guests, and the on looking bodyguards, waiters, and even Anna and the other mistresses were all stunned as the countess held up her cards, admiring them while she celebrated.

Lyu was stunned, too.

Standing stock-still as she gazed in wonder, she looked down at the cards Syr was holding up.

"...So it is."

Not at all clear of what was going on, Lyu immediately readjusted her expression and gave a curt reply.

"Hooray!" Syr was still celebrating like an innocent child.

She had very clearly said the phrase "four of a kind." She had grandly told the table her hand. Terry and the other players were frozen for a few moments before starting to laugh.

It was clearly a bluff.

Total child's play. Pretending to be an aristocrat who doesn't know the ways of the world...a novice who doesn't know the rules of the game.

For the most part, it was clear she would try this kind of bluff. Trying to add pressure with a rule like "*anyone who folds must pay twice the ante*" was just shallow thinking. In the first place, getting four of a kind without changing any cards was obviously not going to happen.

You think I'll fall for that? Terry mocked her in his heart as he secretly signaled with his gaze. Catching the guests' eyes, they exchanged glances. After that, the elderly gentleman animal person waited a second before calling over a waitress.

"Ah, you there. A thirty-year-old Altena wine, please."

Altena wine, thirty years—meaning his hand was a full house with a high-value three of a kind. This round was the old man's win for sure. Using the signals they had decided on, Terry and the other guest pretended to fall for Syr's bluff. The remaining people were just Syr and the animal person.

"It seems it's become a one-on-one fight with this wizened man… what shall we do, madam?"

"Well then, I'll raise."

"Ho-ho-ho! You seem awfully confident there." The old gentleman's lips curved up. He hesitated for a moment, as if thinking about whether to fold before his eyes narrowed. "Very well, then, I shall raise also."

"Raise." Without waiting to exchange cards, Syr pushed out more chips.

"…?!"

She raised again, no trace of uncertainty in her smile. The smiling animal person, Terry, and the other guests stopped moving.

Could it possibly be…? The thought clearly showed in the old man's face before he convinced himself again that it was merely a bluff. His pride wouldn't let him be run in circles by a little girl's strategy.

"Ha, ha-ha-ha…Very well, then let's have the cards decide."

Anger seeping into his smile, the old animal person matched the number of chips Syr had wagered. Lyu stood by, watching quietly as the hands were shown. The old gentleman had a full house.

Against that, Syr had—

"Four of a kind."

Just as she had claimed, she laid down four queens.

"?!"

Her opponents were dumbstruck, seeing a hand that beat the animal person's full house.

"This…T-touché…"

The chips in the pot were pushed over to Syr. The old gentleman gave a smile for appearances while he felt his face burn in humiliation. However, the anger was soon replaced by another emotion.

"This is amazing, dear! Look, they're all the same suit this time!"

"...!"

Again?!

As Syr started talking about her next hand, the guests' faces changed color.

They were enraged, thinking, *As if that could happen a second time!* But also doubtful: *Just maybe...* They were stuck between a rock and a hard place. Pushed into silence, Terry adopted a wait-and-see approach, folding while he watched the other players exchange signs so that the strongest hand would face off against her.

"Ah, it's my win again."

"...!!"

However, it went exactly as she said, and Syr's flush collected all the chips. At that point, the guests' hearts lurched. This girl's luck was strong. They were starting to consider maybe they were being cheated.

"Straight."

Syr stopped putting on a performance. There was no need to hide her true nature anymore. Wearing a beautiful and bold smile, she announced her next hand.

"...F-fold..."

"M-me, too..."

Without testing her claims, all of the guests tried to escape.

It did not end there.

"Three of a kind."

She laid her cards down, revealing her hands.

"Flush."

Quietly, solemnly, audaciously.

"Full house."

Syr ran up consecutive wins, and the platinum-colored chips piled up in front of her. In shock, Terry initially suspected Syr was cheating somehow, or Lyu standing behind her was. He swung his head around. The dealer gasped and furiously shook his head, indicating no. The human bodyguard silently shook his head as well.

Strange...she's too good. The thought echoed in the minds of Terry and his cohorts. Immediately after, as if she had seen through them—

"Ah, that's no good!"

"!"

After winning due to everyone else folding, Syr pushed her cards back facedown to the dealer. This time they slipped out of her hand and ended faceup, only a high card. Watching in shock, the guests' faces turned bright red.

You idiots, she's baiting you!

Terry's flustered internal scream could not reach his accomplices, though.

The furious guests ignored Syr's announcement and challenged her next hand. Immediately after, they all lost. Their mouths gaping wide, the guests could not even speak as looks of utter shock marred their faces. They were in a state of complete confusion.

Shortly after that, the first person dropped out.

"Th-that's..."

The one who retreated was the gentlemanly old animal person who had turned pale from shock. After losing such a massive amount of money, he seemed like a shell of a man. While Terry and the other guests were still stunned, Syr abruptly spoke up as she calmly continued the game.

"Everyone, I'm sure you know, right? Among all the gods and goddesses, there is one goddess who can see the true nature of people's hearts."

"Syr and Lyu are still at the casino, meow? Are they okay, meow?"

At the same time their gamble was happening, in The Benevolent Mistress...

While washing all the plates that had built up in the corner of the kitchen, Ahnya spoke up.

"Worrying is just pointless, meow."

"Yeah, yeah, it would be a bit of a problem if they got mixed up with Ganesha's guys, though. But that's where Lyu will take care of things."

Chloe and Runoa were brushing the concerns off as needless anxiety. The three of them were lined up washing plates as Chloe dejectedly continued,

"Syr's probably already racking up the winnings with an evil smile on that innocent, harmless-looking face, meow..."

She spoke from firsthand experience with Syr's skill at poker, while the other two nodded in agreement.

"How many times have I lost and had to take her place washing dishes, meow?"

"Well, you're hopelessly bad at gambling...but we've never had a chance to win against her."

"It's more than cheap poker faces and bluffs, meow."

Chloe stared at the ceiling as bubbles stuck to her cheek. It was always like that. She would always crush them with a bright smile.

Yeah, it was as if she had read everything in their hands.

"It's as if we were *playing against a god* who could see through our lies..."

With regard to casinos, it was very frowned upon for gods to play poker because they could see through the lies of their "children." Trying to bluff your way through was a lost cause from start to finish—it was that hopeless.

Syr's oddly good instinct was practically at the same level. The catgirls who loved to gamble the most out of all the staff shivered as they recalled it, then sighed.

"Syr is definitely a witch."

"I've heard her eyes can see the smallest of tremors in a heart, laying it entirely bare."

In the shadowy room lit by magic-stone lamps, her slender fingers traced the outline of the cards she had been dealt.

Syr cast her eyes down as she spoke. Her voice almost seemed to have a magical effect, drawing in the people listening.

"Of course, I don't have that goddess's eyes..."

Attracting the guests' eyes single-handedly, Syr stopped and smiled.

"I enjoy it, though. Watching people, that is. There are so many varieties and tons of things to find out...enough to make your eyes sparkle."

Those words resembled something a certain young man had told her.

"Sorry, that's a bad habit of mine," she said without looking the least bit shy. Her eyes, the same silver-blue as her hair, squinted in a bright smile.

"It's something like 'people watching,' I guess? If you keep doing it long enough...somehow or other you can get to the point where you sort of understand, 'This person is thinking about that.'"

Listening to her explanation, it not only applied to the guests she was playing against, but everyone in the VIP room who doubted what they heard.

"Truth or lies, fury or sorrow, shame or suffering...light or darkness."

Was this a bluff, or possibly true? The whirlpool of doubt had already changed into inescapable quicksand. One after the other, the players' expressions shifted. They were sweating as though something had cornered them on the precipice of a sheer cliff. The rich prum went totally pale, unable to keep his hands from trembling.

"Eyes can convey many things."

Standing behind her, Lyu could barely contain the shock she felt. If what she said was true, then Syr was effectively saying she could to read her opponents' thoughts by just looking at their expressions, through the eyes. Announcing her hand, she could see if her opponents wavered just by looking. She raised if they did and drew cards or simply folded when they didn't.

In other words, it was equivalent to knowing her opponents' cards. This was far removed from the experience and strategy Lyu had built up as an adventurer—it was one-sided clairvoyance.

On the one hand it seemed unbelievable, but she also remembered times that Syr's eyes had apparently seen right through to her heart. Without even asking about what was going on, she sometimes came bearing a smile and a solution while Lyu was still struggling to figure out what to do.

"Th-that's…?!"

Terry's cheeks spasmed as he finally lost his cool. She was toying with the one who called himself the king of the gambling paradise and the wealthy elite who had amassed vast riches. A single girl had overwhelmed them. Terry met Syr's gaze. Looking into her eyes, his throat quivered.

What are those metallic-blue eyes seeing?

Why are they twinkling?

What the hell is she hiding behind those eyes?

Hah—what, Countess? What young newlywed? You're a damn witch!!

Terry clenched his right hand, coming to the same conclusion as a certain pair of catgirls. Other than Terry, the guests were running low on chips. At this point, the added rule of "*anyone who folds must pay twice the ante*" was cutting into their lifespans. It had created a situation where they could not wait for a good hand to bring them back from the brink, forcing them to sometimes bluff with weak hands. And Syr always pushed with perfect timing—as if she had foreknowledge that her hands were superior—mercilessly collecting their chips with a cheerful smile.

The first two hands. Those had badly wounded them. That loss had left a decisive mark on them. From the very beginning, they had lost their opportunity to win. One after the other, the guests dropped out, dumbfounded. The game's pace sped up as it entered the final phase. The bodyguards and girls held their breath as the watched.

It was all a strategy.

It was all unfolding in the palm of this girl's hand.

At this rate, I'm going to lose…!

Terry himself had won some of his victories by mere chance, but it was fair to say those times were minimal. But now his own stack of chips had been halved. Countless times, he had been unable to control himself and crushed the cards with his dwarf strength, forcing the dealer to take out a new deck of cards for the next hand.

"!"

At that time, Terry's eyes opened in shock. The first card dealt to him was a chalice symbolizing divine blessing. The next four were four kings. Four of a kind.

The goddess of victory is smiling for me in the end!

Terry rejoiced. With a hand to get his revenge for the first round, it was as if heaven was telling him to win.

Whether you can really see my hand or not doesn't matter now!

All in. He intended to change the flow of the match in one blow here. He glared at Syr with bloodshot eyes. Entrusting himself to the flow of the gamble, he waited for his opponent to step up to the guillotine.

"...Card, please."

In front of the man's glaring, for the first time Syr stopped smiling. She quietly asked to exchange a card. There was a soft rustle as a card was dealt from the deck. Anna gasped even as Terry sneered, tightening the grip on his chips. Eyes from every corner of the VIP room focused on the girl sitting in front of Lyu as she picked up the card.

She placed it into her hand, and the next moment...

"Ha...ha-ha-ha-ahh-ha-ha..."

Seemingly without thinking, she laughed.

"Even though all I did...was think about how nice it would be to borrow some luck." Some heat entered Syr's voice as she closed her eyes, looking like a young girl in love.

Fixing her smile, she opened her eyes and looked at Terry across from her.

Her gaze instantly overpowered him. He heard himself saying, "It's just a bluff—." Believing in his own hand, he pushed everything into the pot. Both players put in a huge amount of chips.

"It seems that I was blessed by a lucky rabbit today," Syr said, just as they were on the verge of showing their cards.

And then she revealed her hand.

"Royal flush."

* * *

Bam! The old animal person stumbled out of his chair and collapsed to the floor. At the impact, Terry's stack of chips collapsed in a cascade. As the platinum chips clinked against each other, the girls covered their mouth with both hands, sweat broke out on the brow of the VIPs, and Anna stood completely still. Everyone in the room stared in shock.

With the inclusion of the wild card, it was the strongest hand of the night.

Terry was so stunned it seemed as though his eyes might leap out of his head as he swung wildly to turn around.

"Faust?!"

In response to the dwarf's roar, the human bodyguard plaintively shook his head.

With his guard telling him that there was no trick, he gritted his teeth as hard as he possibly could.

"Hee-hee, thank you Mr. Rabbit."

Syr picked up the wild card from her hand, a joker riding a *rabbit.* The girl lovingly looked into the *rabbit's* round eyes and, as if remembering the warmth before her separation from the boy, Syr put her hand to her cheek.

"...?!"

The game's winner sat with a mountain of chips in front of her and an elf guard at her back. Having lost all his chips, Terry froze. He had misjudged them. He had no choice but to accept that. At first, he had assumed that the count was a knight who had come to save Anna by himself. But he was wrong. That knight had a guaranteed *trump card* up his sleeve.

The girl in front of him was that trump card—the knight's *queen.*

"Hey, Lyu? This means..."

"Yes, Syr—"

The girl spread her vibrant purple fan clumsily, using both hands.

"—this is your victory."

As Lyu's proclamation echoed, Syr held the fan in front of her mouth, smiling with her blue-silver eyes in front of the shocked wealthy patrons.

© NIRITSU

5

The VIP room was enveloped in silence.

Everyone in the salon stopped moving, all glancing in the same direction in terror. The mountain of chips constructed on the mahogany tabletop. The curtain had closed on the game: an overwhelming victory for one girl. An unimaginable result that would leave anyone shocked, especially the Grand Casino's owner, Terry.

While calmly maintaining the pretense of the count and countess, Lyu and Syr looked over at him.

"Mr. Cervantes, as you promised...will you listen to my husband's request?"

As Syr smiled, Terry clenched his fists tightly. He had promised to fulfill the victor's request before the gamble had started. In front of all the VIPs, not accepting the request would just be a disgrace. Glancing at Anna Kreiz, the flaxen-haired girl at his side, he responded, biting his lip in humiliation.

"Very well...I'll discharge the girl for a little while. Since she just came from a foreign country, I'm sure she is tired."

Terry returned Anna, for whom Lyu had been searching. He seethed as he watched Anna fearfully walk past him, still completely bewildered. In reality, he was letting her go. He had just bought her and hadn't even had the chance to enjoy her yet.

"Are you satisfied, Lord Maximilian?" He spat his words as he stared at the elf who stepped in front of Anna as Syr stood up.

This damn greenhorn...just you watch. You'll regret embarrassing me like this.

While Terry was just barely managing to contain his hatred, Lyu responded.

"No, not yet."

At those words, Terry felt his eyes twitch again in rage.

"...What's that? You aren't satisfied with just Anna?"

Thinking back, he realized that Lyu had never actually said

"Return Anna" as her request. However, asking for more at this point amounted to little more than spite.

Ignoring Terry's expectations, the eye-patch-wearing elf looked straight at him.

"Oh dear, you are quite greedy for an elf, Lord Maximilian. Just how many of my lovers would you have me divorce?"

Ignoring the sarcasm dripping in his words, Lyu responded:

"All of them."

At that, the VIP room instantly fell silent.

"The ones you paid those men to steal. You will free all of these women."

Lyu's pronouncement broke the silence. The women in the room immediately turned around, eyes filled with surprise. Even Syr seemed shocked. Gazing in wonder, her expression gradually changed back to a smile, her shoulders starting to shake as she suppressed a giggle.

"My dear husband certainly is greedy. Hee-hee."

The blue-and-silver-haired girl giggled, her mood somewhere between happiness and hilarity.

"...Y-you...!"

Stunned, Terry's face turned a purplish red, his anger breaking through the shock. Slowly rising to his feet, the dwarf's stony face was menacing with no further attempts to hide his true nature.

"Don't get ahead of yourself, greenhorn..."

His threatening voice was unsuited to the VIP room.

As rage tinged his eyes, Anna, the girls, and the VIPs cowered.

"Maybe you're misunderstanding something? Who do you think you are? All you did is win one game!"

"..."

"Do you really think you'll survive if you make an enemy of me?! If you think the Guild will protect you, you've made a big mistake! I can just go back to Santorio Vega if—"

"Wrong."

Lyu quietly interrupted his threats.

"You aren't a citizen of Santorio Vega. Your name isn't Terry Cervantes, either."

The dwarf froze.

"Your name is Ted."

At that declaration, the man's face changed drastically.

"In the past, you were the bookie for an establishment that repeatedly ran illegal gambling dens in Orario…Even though the goddess you contracted with was exiled from Orario and returned to the heavens, that Status is still engraved on your back."

Lyu took a small vial containing a scarlet liquid and fragment of crystal. Status Thief was an item that revealed the Status engraved by a god onto their faction. When used, the identity of a person's patron deity and their *real name* would appear on their back as proof. Lyu held out the vial to back up her assertion.

A strange mood took over the VIP room. As if the room had frozen over, no one moved a muscle. Left in the lurch, the guests, girls, and even the waiters looked on in confusion as the elf and dwarf stared at each other.

"…Ho…ho-ho. That a pretty wild accusation you're making there."

Finally, the owner opened his mouth. He was striking a calm pose, but there was a hint of unease in his voice that had not been present before. At the same time, his glare was overflowing with bloodlust.

"I have no intention of wasting my time with pointless delusions… More importantly, I can't allow people who go around impugning me or the reputation of this establishment with nonsense stories to leave alive."

Terry raised his hand, and the men who had been loitering moved at his signal. Starting with a murmur, a large commotion roiled around the room. Black-suited men surrounded Syr and Lyu. The hired guards followed his orders obediently, driving away the flustered old animal person, the rich prum, and the other participants away from the table with a sharp glance.

He intended to eliminate the Status Thief item—along with the one who had made the allegations about his identity.

"Once…yes, just once before I kill you, tell me who you really are, you bastard," Terry demanded, smothering his agitation.

As Anna cowered, Lyu held out her hand to Syr.

"You don't remember me?"

She took the stole from out of Syr's arms. Using the long, narrow cloth, she wrapped it like a turban. Other than her uncovered right eye, her entire face was covered. A puzzled look appeared on Terry's face—then as he stared into the one uncovered eye, he gasped. He started sweating heavily.

"I-it can't be—"

A sky-blue eye peered out from inside the stole, a *veiled look* that matched someone in his memories. The sharp gaze pierced through him, and the next instant he shouted in a loud voice:

"—Leon?!"

An adventurer who had once made villains quiver at the sound of her name: *Leon of the Gale Wind.*

A notorious second-tier adventurer who always wore a veil to cover her face and whose identity was never discovered. Someone whose strength could even be compared to the Sword Princess's. The executioner of justice who had condemned more evil than anyone else in *Astrea Familia.*

It was her second coming. The color drained from Terry's face as the follower of the goddess Astrea revealed herself.

"You're alive…?! That means, you really were in that War Game…?!"

Terry had heard that Gale Wind had turned to revenge after losing her comrades in the familia but had been mercilessly killed in the battle with the target of her fury. A corpse was never discovered, but Terry had believed the rumors when Gale Wind stopped roaring through the city.

Until today.

"I heard rumors that you were back, using a false name."

The beautiful elf woman in men's clothes stared at Terry as she removed the veil. Lyu had vaguely suspected that the dwarf she had once chased down had changed his name and appearance and resurfaced in the Casino Strip. As she gathered more information and learned more of his characteristics, she had a sense of déjà vu at the modus operandi. And when they met face-to-face today in the casino's hall, she was sure of it.

"Did you ever wonder why I overlooked your evil deeds?"

Lyu's eyes narrowed as the dwarf's heart pounded, his mouth opening and closing silently.

"There were two reasons. The first is that I don't have the right to talk about justice. And the other is..." Her eyes widened as she raised her voice.

"...Goddess Astrea offered you one more chance when you prostrated yourself, begging for forgiveness."

Terry's—or rather, Ted's—face paled.

When he was younger, he had dirtied his hands with crime and been caught in a roundup of criminals by *Astrea Familia.* Caught red-handed, Ted had fallen down in front of the goddess and put his forehead to the ground, begging to be spared. The goddess Astrea listened to his request with compassion. Perhaps she wanted to believe in the children's ability to improve and rehabilitate, hoping that the residents of the mortal realm who were not eternal might change.

Lyu laid bare her fury at this man who was only free due to the goddess's kindness and yet still cultivated more evil in service of his selfish desires.

"G-get her already!"

Ted finally shouted as he stood under a just gaze that had not weakened after all these years. Having lost his composure, he ordered his bodyguards to dispose of Lyu.

"There is no more room for leniency with you."

The sturdy men advanced to pin her from all sides, but she easily knocked them back.

"Gah!"

"Guh!"

While moving in a circle covering Syr and Anna, she used kicks to send their large bodies crashing into the wall and the table.

As the bodyguards who had fallen victim to her techniques hit the floor, the female VIPs in the room cried out.

"I'll judge you in her stead."

In an instant, screams filled the VIP room. Trembling in terror in the center of the noisy room, Ted finally pulled out his trump card, no longer carrying about appearances.

"Faust! Lolo! Kill her!"

At their employer's order, the two bodyguards standing behind him moved—a medium built, burly human and a slim catman. As the two men came rushing toward her, Lyu's expression tightened.

"Syr, take her and get back."

Her eyes signaled that she would not have enough leeway to protect them as she leaped into the fray, challenging the skilled fighters coming to attack her.

"Okay. Good luck, Lyu."

Closing the distance in an instant, the human and catman drew their specialized weapons.

Black steel gauntlets and two knives. As the enemy made contact, unleashing a sharp punch and slash, Lyu leaped over their heads, avoiding their attack. Landing behind them, she immediately kicked at their heads.

"!"

The black gauntlet repelled her kick, and the knife swung in from the side with perfect timing. Twisting her body to dodge, Lyu's formal outfit was lightly cut.

"Faust and Lolo are the famous Black Fist and Black Cat! I'm sure you've heard of them before!"

Watching the ebb and flow of their fight, Ted wiped his sweat and smiled ferociously. Lyu knew the names well. They were the aliases of a menacing bounty hunter and an assassin.

From a time when *Astrea Familia* was still alive, the Dark Age when the Evils ran rampant in Orario, countless bounty hunters and assassins had been hired from outside the city in order to dispose of wanted men and enemies. Guided by Guild members who colluded with the Evils, they invaded the Labyrinth City and, like mercenaries, they determined their enemies and allies based on their reward, becoming one of the sources of turmoil in the city.

Among them, the names and strength of Black Fist and Black Cat resounded through the underworld. Their contract success rate was basically one hundred percent. Their names became a synonym for terror at the time, having even fulfilled contracts on second-tier adventurers.

When Orario's Dark Age came to a close, like Lyu they had disappeared.

I see, they're strong...

She acknowledged the might of the two men in front of her, while ignoring Ted's boasts that they had been at his side since the Dark Age. These two had the skills to prevent a Level 4 like her from attacking carelessly. They combined their moves flawlessly.

Quickly and accurately analyzing the situation, they aimed for her eye patch—her weak point—constantly alternating attacks from the blind spot it created.

If I take the eye patch off, I might be able to get in a surprise attack... but first I need a weapon.

The bodyguards reentered the fray from the front and back while Lyu was unarmed and under pressure from her enemies' weapons.

"While they're pinning him down...!" the dwarf snapped with a husky voice that had lost all composure.

Ted could not relax as he watched Lyu go toe-to-toe with Faust and Lolo. The scariness of *Astrea Familia* had seeped into his bones.

"You waiters, grab Anna and that woman!!"

The waiters from Santorio Vega were flustered but did not disobey as he ordered them to get hostages. Shady though he may be, the owner's orders were absolute.

As the surrounding guests kept screaming, they corralled Syr and Anna near the wall.

"Uh...ummm...?!"

"..."

Anna became fearful as the ring of people closed in around them and Syr quietly took in the situation with the waiters. She surveyed the surroundings, ignoring Anna's gaze that seemed to be urging Syr to just leave her behind and escape.

Lyu did not react to them. Trusting her colleague, she just focused on her own fight.

Finally, without any warning, Syr raised both of her hands. A sharp noise rang out as she clapped her hands once in front of her chest.

"!"

Shocked at the loud, sudden noise, the waiters stopped moving, and even the other people nearby focused on her. Remembering the mysteriousness she displayed in the game just a little while before, they unconsciously readied themselves as Syr spoke in a restaurant staff's voice that carried well in the crowd, smiling with her hands together.

"Everyone who was kidnapped by this awful owner: You aren't just caged birds waiting for the hero to save you, are you?"

The mistresses, who had been left standing in confusion as the situation took such an unforeseen turn, were shocked when the idea of escaping was brought up.

Talking to those girls, Syr continued.

"You don't look that way to me. You are all very strong people. People who didn't lose to adversity. Because you all are pure and have a determined spirit. I know you all have people waiting for you."

The women's eyes wavered, as if they were remembering who they used to be. With each word, Syr stirred up a longing for freedom in their hearts.

"Also, if that hero wins...everyone will be free."

She pointed to the eye-patch-wearing elf who was even now fighting the bodyguards. Watching the elf gallantly fight, the women's eyes, which had been dyed with resignation, brightened, and then filled with the pent-up fury along they had accumulated. Seeing that, Syr smiled brightly.

"So let's run wild! ♪"

Once she had lit the fuse, it exploded in the blink of an eye. The girls screamed in one voice:

"Uaaaaaaaaaaaaaaaaaaaaaaa!"

"I'm going home, meow!"

The women who had been beautiful dolls roared in anger, recklessly getting violent. The waiters turned pale. Unlike the bodyguards Lyu had downed, they did not have particular confidence in their strength. Fighting against the number of women Ted had gathered into his so-called collection was hopeless from the start. Humans leaped in, ignoring their dresses, elves haphazardly threw sparkling chips, and animal girls scratched up the faces of waiters that they caught. Capturing Syr or Anna was hopeless. Their opponents were knocked down at the feet of the dumbfounded guests, who cried out in shock.

As the women's rebellion spread across the VIP room, shouts rang out.

"Wh-wh…what?!"

Ted's entire face started twitching as the riot unfolded before his eyes.

"…Wh-who are…?"

"?"

Anna's flaxen hair trembled as she seemingly struggled not to fall over backward at the scene unfolding before her eyes. Syr tilted her head slightly as the girl timidly opened her mouth.

"Who are you people?"

"…"

"Why? You've never met us…"

Anna had been looking at Syr and turned her gaze to Lyu. Placing a hand on her breast, Syr also watched the elf resolutely fighting.

"Well, I'm just tagging along, but…Lyu wanted to help in whatever way possible after hearing your story. Lyu likes to put up a front, but it's really just that, I think."

Anna inhaled sharply and clutched her chest as the woman standing next to her continued her monologue.

"Don't be mistaken, Lyu is not some hero of justice without past mistakes."

Speaking clearly, her platinum eyes narrowed.

"However…I like that kind side."

And then she smiled broadly. Syr's whispers were drowned out as Lyu's battle sped up.

"—I can't take it anymore!"

Crying people appeared everywhere as the VIP room turned into a battlefield. The exhausted wealthy prum ran at full speed from the midst of the guests. Deciding to take the opportunity, the scratched-up old chienthrope gentleman and the other guests followed him. They ran for the large oaken doors, the exit from the VIP room.

"Call *Ganesha Familia*!"

"Hurry up!"

"Oy, watch what you're doing!"

As the guests panicked, Ted's angry shouts telling them to stop were drowned out. Once Lyu was silenced, he could use however much money and influence were necessary to make this go away, but he really did not want things to get rougher. Unnecessarily inviting suspicion by bringing the city in for help was his absolute last resort.

It was the same for Lyu. For someone on the blacklist, trying to accuse the owner of not being from Santorio Vega would not be believable. If *Ganesha Familia* showed up, their first step would be to ensure the safety of the guests and the owner. If Ted escaped in the three-way struggle, she would not be able get to him again. She did not want *Ganesha Familia* to get involved. However, she had to let it go. Glancing aside at the flood of guests looking for help, she continued her battle. And also, she had faith that *someone* in *Ganesha Familia* would do something about him for her.

The tide first began to turn with the gatekeepers flanking the oaken doors.

"…?"

"What was that—something with the VIP room?"

Some of the guests enjoying themselves gambling in the hall noticed the two guards moved toward the center of the doorway. Tilting their heads, they wondered if something had happened. After just a little bit of time passed—*BAM! BAM!* It sounded like someone was ramming the door. The sudden noise startled the people approaching the area in front of the doors, and the next instant…

"Uwwwaaaaaaaaaaaaaaaaaa!"

Pushing aside the waiters and gatekeepers, the VIPs overflowed from inside the room.

"?!"

As people heard the screams, they turned, one after the other, in shock. The highest-status guests in the gambling paradise, the ones who had been invited to the VIP room, were flinging decorum to the wind as they struggled to be the first out of the room.

"What happened?!"

"I dunno, but move it!"

While the people and gods farther away from the VIP room made a stir trying to figure out what was going on, *Ganesha Familia* immediately sprang into action.

The guards they had provided wove through the gaps in the crowd as they cut toward the VIP room. Then…

"—this asshole!"

Wild shouts rang out.

What now?! the members of *Ganesha Familia* thought. If they turned around, they would see disreputable men wrestling. Adventurers were scuffling with each other. Without any concern for the trouble going on around them, they started fighting. The casino employees had no reason to stop stupid guests arguing with each other. Their cries of anguish turned into a riot.

Shocked, the *Ganesha Familia* members came to a stop.

"Uooooooooooo! What are we doing?!!!!!!!!!!"

"Hell if I know!!!!!!!!"

—Scott and Guile from Mord's crew were crying as they grappled. Mord himself was next to them, grabbing a white-haired boy.

"Damn it!!!!!!!!! We're gonna get banned!! Why, Little Rookie?!!!!!!!!!!!!"

"I-I'm sorryyy!"

The riot happening now was Bell's—or more accurately Syr's—suggestion to slow down *Ganesha Familia.*

"This VIP room is a place that even members of Ganesha Familia *may not enter."*

"So no one can come in."

"Even if something happens, no one can come in here."

Syr had whispered that to him when he had been called to the VIP room. That was the message from her and Lyu: *No matter what happens, no one can be allowed to get close to the VIP room.* Somehow understanding the message, Bell had asked Mord's group for help, which confused them greatly. "Somehow or other I need to do something. Please help me." They absolutely refused, but when they heard it was for Lyu, to whom they owed a favor for the fight on the eighteenth floor, they tearfully gave in.

"You must be some kind of jinx, you bastard!!!!"

"I'm sooooooooooorrrrryyyyyyyyyy!"

As Mord got more desperate, he threw Bell through the air in an attention-grabbing display, and the boy's body landed neatly splayed across a table. Several tables were overturned as a rain of chips danced through the air. The dealers turned pale and cowered as a human manager who came to stop them was sent flying just like Bell.

Guests frantically trying to avoid the mayhem crashed into each other and knocked each other away. Greedy gods feverishly gathered the chips scattered across the floor. In an instant, the entire hall fell into chaos.

"Wh-where should we go…?!"

Momentarily trapped between the chaos inside the VIP room and Mord's group's riot behind them, the *Ganesha Familia* members hesitated.

"Wh-what are you doing?! Hurry up and clear up the disorder in the hall!"

A fat elf with sweat dripping from his brow, Royman Mardeel's shout was the deciding factor. The faction members were forced to prioritize the suppression of the main hall at the demand of the Guild chief, who was desperate to prevent Orario's reputation from dropping. Since the chaos in the casino showed no signs of dying down, the relief for the VIP room would be substantially delayed.

A handful of remaining waiters were desperately trying to resist the women's revolt. The furious battle of Falna-blessed warriors raged on in the middle area of the VIP room.

"!"

Lyu dodged the skillfully coordinated twin attacks. Two versus one. Not only that, she was staving off brutal gauntlets and fierce knife slashes while empty-handed. She was clearly an opponent wielding high-level Technique and Strategy.

—This elf is strong.

—It's really Gale Wind.

The men were dubious at first, but their hearts whispered that they were fighting a truly strong person. Calmly analyzing their opponent's strength, the two bodyguards attacked repeatedly without giving an opportunity for a counterattack.

"Level Three, right?"

While defending, Lyu also saw through their true strength. She whispered to herself as the bottom of her shoe flew through the air and struck the enemy's gauntlet, and she used the combined force of the kick and punch to jump back and open significant space between them. As the elf tried to reestablish some range, the human and cat-person prepared themselves without letting their guard down.

"You certainly have real strength...but you're just like your owner."

"?"

Looks of suspicion floated across the bodyguard's faces as Lyu spoke up to them.

"You are faking your identity. You aren't Black Fist or Black Cat."

Their faces twisted in shock at her declaration. As her assertion rang out in the room, Anna wasn't the only one surprised as she watched the fight with bated breath—even Ted doubted his ears.

"You match the names, but Black Fist and Black Cat were individualists who never trusted anyone other than themselves for contracts. Obviously, they would not have fought in a large group, but they also assuredly would never have worked together with the coordination you two have."

She spoke as if she had fought the *real thing* before. The elf standing there was Gale Wind, a person of true strength who had survived the city's Dark Age, so objectively speaking, that was entirely believable. The human and catperson bodyguards gritted their teeth as her disinterested gaze seemed to say, *Your real strength has risen plenty on its own, so why strut around with a borrowed reputation?*

"...Sha!"

As if enraged that their deception had been exposed, the men assaulted Lyu. In this monster-filled Labyrinth City, they were not worth considering, so they had survived by polishing their teamwork and coordination, which they used to pummel the opponent in front of their eyes.

The intensity of their offense and defense increased severalfold. The instant the fake Black Fist led the enemy to defend, the catperson dove in from Lyu's blind spot, the left side where the eye patch obstructed her vision.

You're mine! The man was sure of himself.

"—Wh—!"

He saw a leather shoe about to hit his body, and his confidence changed to a tremor. Without looking at him, she hit him with a ferocious kick from below his line of sight as he put his hand on the floor.

—A trap.

She had purposefully used the eye patch's blind spot as a lure. She dangled it as bait and invited him to dive into her range. And the catperson ate a deadly kick, having fallen it for it just as Lyu predicted.

"Guh?!"

"Sharl?!"

The foot connected with the catperson's jaw and launched him away. Both of his knives slipped out of his hands, and his body rolled across the floor as it hit. A direct strike from a Level 4 kick.

He was totally knocked out with one attack. The human who had called his partner Sharl was stunned as Lyu easily walked toward him and picked up the two blades.

"Black Fist and Black Cat both had a Status of Level Four." The human gulped as Lyu thrust her words at him.

"In addition to that, Faust and Lolo were not code names, they were real names."

Holding the unsheathed blades in a reverse grip, Lyu walked straight forward.

Just who is this elf? All he did was pick up a weapon, but I feel so much more pressure, and he knows way too much about that bounty hunter and assassin. Those thoughts were conveyed in his cold sweat.

"—Most importantly, Black Fist and Black Cat were *women*."

The man went wide-eyed at a third shock.

"They are currently working to earn a day's income at a tavern that I'm also indebted to."

At the same time…

In a tavern far away from the casino, a human and a catgirl were at work washing dishes. Runoa Faust and Chloe Lolo each let out a large sneeze.

"U—uaaaaaaaaaaaaaaa!"

As if losing himself, he roared. The man stealing the name Black Fist lashed out.

As her opponent approached her, swinging his black steel gauntlets, Lyu moved even faster, the two blades gleaming.

Her knives flashed. Eight in all. As he passed behind Lyu, his gauntlets fell to the ground like wooden building blocks. Multiple slashes were engraved on his arms.

"—"

An attack speed worthy of the name Gale Wind. Time seemed to freeze for the man as blood drops scattered from the sharp knife wounds. Lyu did not stop there. Closing in on him again, she spun, mercilessly unleashing a spinning kick to his head.

"—Guah!"

His body was sent flying with the force of a river breaking its dam to crash into a wall. The thunderous sound returned the VIP room to silence as the women and waiters pulled back, no longer moving. The human and catman lay on the floor, unconscious. As the women looked on in shock, the main battle concluded.

"You're lucky you fought me. If the people whose names you borrowed were here, you wouldn't have gotten off so easily."

Lyu gave her unconscious enemies a warning out of concern.

"A-amazing..."

Anna expressed wonder mixed with fear at how the battle had unfolded. She was captivated as the gallant elf glanced over at her, displaying an amazing strength worthy of a fairy-tale hero. Then—

"—Come!!"

"Kyaa!"

A thick hand clutched her slender arm. Ted had been watching the battle, and the moment he recognized that the bodyguards' defeat was imminent, he hid his presence and snuck close to Anna. Wielding a dwarf's peculiar strength, he yanked her away in one motion as if she weighed no more than a feather. As Syr turned in shock, the two disappeared down a passage leading deeper into the VIP room.

"Lyu!"

"I'll follow. Stay here!"

Before Syr could even speak, Lyu was already dashing away. She knew that, as quick on her feet as Syr was, she could get away by passing as one of the mistresses whenever *Ganesha Familia* came into the VIP room and questioned her. Leaving her friend in a safe spot, Lyu chased after Ted and Anna.

The drama had reached at its final stage.

6

They ran down the hallway, their footsteps thumping along the extravagant carpet. Large beads of sweat seeping from every pore, the dwarf Ted dragged Anna along as he fled deeper and deeper into the casino. All of the bodyguards he had employed had been wiped out. All of his pawns had been blown away in the VIP room. He was the king of the gambling paradise, wasn't he? Until just a little while ago, he was. But now, at the hands of a single elf, he was forced to flee in humiliation.

"They faked their names! What Black Fist?! What Black Cat?! Those bastards!"

Already forgetting that he had been also been caught faking his identity, the owner shouted at the bodyguards for which he had paid a huge sum of money. He was no longer pretending to be Terry Cervantes. All that was left was the criminal Ted.

"Ah-ahhhhh…!"

As the man got angrier, his grip tightened, and a moan escaped Anna's lips. Even now, she was desperately resisting, but the strength of a dainty young girl was like that of a baby in comparison to a dwarf's superhuman strength.

He dragged his insurance forcefully along with him, lifting her legs off the floor at times. A fierce beat of footsteps and a violent presence were hot on their heels.

"Grr—!"

As Lyu bore down on them, Ted jumped in desperation, hounded by fear and unease. It was a gaudy, long hallway decorated by crude bronze statues and paintings. Passing room after room assigned to the women, they headed into the casino's back rooms, then the backyard, passing shocked dealers and staff as they went.

"Mr. Cervantes, what are you doing?!"

"What's all this…?!"

"Stop the elf behind me!!"

Without giving the stunned staff and remaining bodyguards any semblance of an explanation, Ted kept running. The area he had just passed through erupted into a loud struggle, and then cries rang out, stoking Ted's fear. With Bell's group in the main hall, and now this, both sides of the Grand Casino of El Dorado Resort were descending into a never-before-seen chaos.

"Here!"

Swinging Anna around painfully, he changed their path to wind countless times across the labyrinthine backyard before they ran down a long staircase. The casino's underground floor.

It did not have any of the splendor of the main hall where games were played, but it was just as large as the aboveground floor in size. Raising his voice, he repeatedly told the flustered, staring people to open the enclosing wall as he exited onto a wide, long path. At the end of the path was a giant round metal door. The Grand Casino's underground vault.

"Faster! Faster…!"

Almost as if he was planning to ram the door, he ran toward it, his fingers trembled as he took out a master key that only he possessed. Opening all the locks, he spun the handle like the captain of a ship, swinging the giant metal door out. His face was bright red. Having opened the door, he pushed Anna into the vault and slipped in himself.

"Ha…ha…if I come here…!"

Thunk. The metal door slammed shut. Anna looked around from where she had collapsed on the floor as the sound of the locks closing echoed in the room. Polished gold coins were everywhere. The inside of the vault was like a small cottage, filled with all the money deposited at the casino. There were innumerable mountains of gold, and each appeared to contain at least a hundred million coins. An incomprehensibly large amount of money.

All of the Grand Casino's commodities were stored here. It was El Dorado Resort's treasure box—Anna gasped at this room, which befitted a place that billed itself as The Golden City.

"The only one who can open this vault is me, and it's made from adamantite from the Dungeon! He can't get in or break in!"

As he caught his breath, a smile finally formed on Ted's face. As he had said, the vault was made from adamantite mined in the Dungeon. He had sourced large amounts of the rare metal from merchants and familias to build it, heedless of the needs of others. In order to protect against skilled thief familias, it was a small underground fortress. Ted's aim was to hole up in this underground vault.

"As long as I'm cooped up in here, even Leon can't do anything about it. *Ganesha Familia* will capture him eventually, since he's already on the blacklist."

"...!"

"Until then...Anna, I'll have you keeping me company to soothe me."

Ted looked up, his eyes bloodshot.

"They keep getting in my way. I can't hold the rage back anymore!"

"Ngh...?!"

"*Astrea Familia*, those ghosts from the past! I'm the one getting the last laugh!!"

His clothes were stained with sweat, his slicked-back hair a mess. Ted unleashed his sadism, intending to take out all his pent-up resentment on the girl in front of him.

"Acting cute while making a fool of me...It's just a shame he won't be able to hear your screams..."

"S-stop!"

The dwarf's shadow started toward the trembling girl. Her flaxen hair shook in terror. Sensing danger, she reflexively scooted away from him.

"Hmph!"

"Guah!"

An animal person rolled to the floor, struck by a boot to the cheek. After her swift kick, Lyu sprinted forward. She proceeded through the underground floor, instantly dealing with the waves of guards who attacked her. From the aboveground floor through the stairway, countless demi-humans were laid out along the path she had taken. She ran past them like the wind in order to reclaim the girl whom Ted had stolen from her family.

"That's..."

Breaking through the last door, she emerged onto a wide path. At the edge of her vision, she saw the vault where Ted had holed up. Lyu's eyes narrowed as she stopped in front of the haughty adamantite door, the seal on the metal castle wall.

"*—Distant forest sky. Infinite stars inlaid upon the eternal night sky.*"

She started chanting.

"This is...magic?"

As he was about to lash out at Anna, Ted noticed the flow of magic being wielded from far behind him. The swirling torrent of power was strong enough for him to perceive it, even shut off from external stimuli inside the vault. As he whirled around, his face broke into a sneer.

"Bwa-ha-ha-ha! That's pointless, Leon!! Even you can't break this vault! That isn't about to change even if you use magic!"

The dwarf's husky laughter echoed off the mountains of gold coins.

"*Heed this foolish one's voice, and once more grant the starfire's divine protection.*"

Lyu walked forward steadily, with an air of composure, her footsteps ringing out. Her beautiful chanting voice did not hesitate in the slightest. Her mantra echoed cool and clear as she added more force to her voice.

"*Grant the light of compassion to the one who forsook you.*"

"Ha-ha-ha-ha...?"

The loud laughter echoing in the vault died down. That enormous amount of magic. It was as though he were standing in front of a cannon loading an especially large *cannonball.*

"O…oh…?"

Even a normal person like Anna could feel the power welling on the other side of the vault. She went wide-eyed as Ted's sneering face twitched.

"Come, wandering wind, fellow traveler."

Lyu pulled her tie off, letting it drop to the floor as she loosened her collar. Her throat quivered, speeding up the spell as she advanced.

"Cross the skies and sprint through the wilderness, swifter than anything—"

She refined her Mind, infusing the source of magic. The undulating power that was gathering in front of her converged the instant before it was released. Stopping to leave a bit of distance, Lyu stared at the metal door with her sky-blue right eye.

"*—Imbue the light of stardust and strike down my enemy.*"

Accompanied by flashes of wind and stars, she thrust her right arm forward like a conductor. The chanting complete, Lyu quietly spoke the name of her trump card, the strongest sure-kill spell.

"Luminous Wind."

Clothed in wind, a cannon blast of starlight rang out.

"~~~~~~~~~~~~?!"

Stardust rushing through the sky turned into several large light spheres, accompanied by a green wind, that hit the vault. A string of billowing explosions rang out through the underground. Wave after wave of shocks and awe-inspiring explosions washed over Ted and Anna. As they ducked, the door made of numerous layers of adamantite bent inward, cracks forming.

"———"

As Ted stood frozen in place, Anna suddenly lay flat on the ground. The next instant, the vault exploded with an enormous boom.

"—Whaaaaaaaaaaa?!"

His vision overwhelmed by a flash of white light, Ted's frozen form was blown back. Because of the shock wave, the mountains of gold coins were also scattered in the air, turning into countless gold raindrops, clinking loudly as they splashed across the floor.

When Anna lifted her head, she saw that half of the vault's door had been torn away.

"Adamantite's hardness is directly proportional to its purity."

Emerging from the smoke, Lyu stepped into the large hole in the underground vault.

"If it were the rare metal from the *deep levels*—the highest purity adamantite—then it would certainly have been exceedingly difficult to break through."

Anna and Ted—who was somehow pulling himself up—both gazed at her in terror as she spoke.

"However, the materials to make this clearly were excavated from the *upper* and *middle levels*...If it is lower-strength adamantite, then my magic can pierce it.

"You obtained *inferior goods*," Lyu explained as she glanced at Ted, who had lost his voice.

Telling the difference was impossible for someone who was neither a smith nor an upper-class adventurer. Arrogantly throwing around money had only bought him the resentment of the merchants, who paid him back with this meager revenge.

Ted's face colored in shock at his miscalculation, and his cheeks quivered as Lyu calmly approached.

"L-Leon..."

His clothes ragged, Ted's tongue spasmed as his gaze shifted to the side. Anna was there, still unable to stand up. The next instant, he leaped, reaching out to grab her. However, faster than a dwarf could move, the elf's hand whisked the girl away.

"...?!"

"Time to grit your teeth, you beast," Lyu calmly announced as she looked down at the cowering dwarf.

The handsome elf wrapped one arm around Anna's waist as she

blushed, moving in front of the girl to cover her. Lyu was wearing just a single dress glove.

"Damn…Daaaaaaaamn!"

As his eyes flashed, she clenched her bare fist.

"I should tell you—I won't hold back." Measuring the distance carefully, she smashed Ted's cheek with an unforgiving gale-force attack.

"Gahhhh?!"

The tremendous force behind Lyu's fist hurled the dwarf into a collapsing mountain of gold coins, which scattered further. Half-buried in gold, the villainous dwarf twitched and moaned. The elf who would not touch the skin of people she did not acknowledge tossed the glove she had removed at Ted.

"Let's go."

"Eh? But…"

"*Ganesha Familia* will take care of the rest. As long as the women who heard my story testify, he won't escape interrogation."

Turning her back on Ted, she called to Anna, who was still lost. The flaxen-haired beauty walked out with Lyu but suddenly stopped.

"Um…"

"?"

As Lyu turned around, the girl clasped her hands in front of her chest, her pure white dress shifting.

"You went so far for me when we've never met and don't know each other…Thank you very much."

"…You aren't hurt, are you?"

"Eh? Ah…n-no."

"Good."

Lyu smiled slightly, encouraging the trembling girl to calm down. Anna's eyes instantly welled up, and she gasped a bit as she looked down. Lyu tilted her head a bit at the odd reaction.

"Lyu!"

"Syr?"

Holding the hem of her dress, Syr appeared in the vault.

"Why are you here?"

"I followed the trail of bodies in the corridor and caught up to you two."

"...I thought I was clear that you should stay there."

Syr stuck out her tongue as Lyu sighed. Anna kept fidgeting as if she were uncomfortable between the two of them.

"—Leon!!"

At that point, a hoarse voice called out. Ted's. While the others were turned away, the dwarf had regained consciousness, screaming as he shakily tried to stand up.

"You think I'll go down like this?! I'm bringing you down with me!"

"..."

"I'll use my underlings to spread rumors until you're caught! You *are* in the city! Ha-ha-ha-ha! Everyone with a grudge will be looking for you. Don't dare think you'll get a moment of peace!"

Ted burned with hatred, his cheek smashed, blood flowing out of his mouth and staining his clothes. He climbed to his knees, glaring at Lyu as he swore to bring her down with him as revenge. Instead of Lyu, the one who moved to close his mouth was the platinum-haired girl. She listened quietly to his speech as she approached him.

"Wh-what?! What are you doing?!"

Ted was disturbed, remembering the mysterious ability she displayed in the poker game. Syr did not say anything, just smiled brilliantly. She bent at the waist and Ted instinctively flinched as she moved her face close to his ear to whisper something.

"—"

After a second he turned unnaturally stiff, his mouth opening and closing over and over again as if he was struggling to breathe. Facing the dwarf man who was looking up at her in shock, she smiled again. Ted fell back to the ground, this time as if all his strength had finally left him.

"Let's go, Lyu!"

"..."

Lyu wanted to ask what she said, but there was no time. If they waited here, *Ganesha Familia* would show up. For the present, they left Ted and hurried away out of the underground vault.

"Syr...what did you say at the end?"

After they climbed the stairs and escaped the underground floor, running down the passageways without meeting anyone, Lyu asked her question. The blue-and-silver-haired girl smiled like a child playing a prank.

"I said the name of the familia of our benefactor, Mama Mia."

Hearing those words, Lyu was dumbstruck. At the same time, ever so slightly, she sympathized with Ted. The owner of The Benevolent Mistress, the restaurant that they lived under, was none other than Mia Grand. She was half-retired, but she was still a member of a certain familia—.

The underground vault was thoroughly destroyed.

The sound of multiple footsteps overlapped as finally *Ganesha Familia* arrived on the scene. Ted still sat on the floor in a daze. Under the suspicious gazes of the faction members, he incoherently muttered a single phrase over and over.

"*F-Freya Familia*..."

Letting the frantic staff rush past them, Lyu's group set out for the casino's back entrance. They kept seeing people who had left their posts in the backyard because of the unexpected turn of events, which allowed them to proceed smoothly. Using the pandemonium, they arrived successfully at the back entrance.

"Apparently the people who started the uproar in the VIP room were pretending to be aristocrats!"

"It was an elf and human pair—don't let them go!"

"!"

However, adventurers were ready and waiting at the back door. *Ganesha Familia* was definitely top-class, getting there so quickly. They had immediately grasped the situation and surrounded the casino, establishing a perimeter that not even an ant could sneak through. At the back of the establishment they had just left was a giant pool that could only be found in the Casino Strip.

The blue water's surface reflected the moonlit sky and sparkled under the magic-stone lamps. Sheltering Syr and Anna behind her, Lyu scrutinized the scene as all the *Ganesha Familia* members scattered around were on guard, watching.

"Did you catch the intruder?"

"Chief Shakti!"

—At that point, the second thing that Lyu had not predicted happened. The person who had been granted the second name *Ankusha* by the gods, the strongest first-tier adventurer in *Ganesha Familia*, arrived.

Her azure hair was cut short above her shoulders. With long arms and legs, she was tall for a woman at more than 170 celches tall. She was human, but she had a sagacious bearing that would fit the extensive knowledge of an elf.

This beautiful woman, wearing a suit that resembled a dealer's, ran over and signaled to the faction members.

"I'll take it from here."

"Eh? But..."

"It seems like there aren't enough people, so you and your people should go help out near the establishment."

"Understood!"

As an expression of trust, the top-class adventurers readily changed positions according to the chief's orders.

As Syr and Anna watched in shock, the members left them. When only the woman was left, she glanced over at the girls that Lyu was hiding.

"Get out."

Lyu stepped out.

"Shakti..."

"I heard that an elven thief had snuck in...but it was really this, eh?"

While watching Lyu as she started moving forward, *Ganesha Familia*'s chief—Shakti Varma—sighed as if she had predicted this.

Shakti and Lyu were acquaintances. When the Evils ran unchecked in Orario's Dark Age, they had built a friendship when Lyu had worked with *Ganesha Familia* who protected the peace and order of the city just like *Astrea Familia*. Shakti was one of a very small number of people who knew both Lyu's face and that she was still alive and living in Orario.

Even now, she was one of the strongest in the city, having become a hero. She sighed as she peered at Anna, who nervously stepped out from behind Lyu.

"We put so much work into figuring out how to round up the casino management for their barbarity, and it's gone up in smoke now..."

She stared at the shimmering surface of the pool for a second. As Shakti turned back to Lyu and the rest, she closed her eyes.

"I didn't see anything. Not a wanted person with a mob after them, not a Robin Hood rescuing a kidnapped girl...nothing."

Lyu's eyes went wide as she heard those words. Catching her breath, she took Syr and Anna with her, leaving the unpopulated poolside.

"Thank you, Shakti."

"It's fine, so go."

As she passed beside her, Lyu expressed her gratitude and slipped a small vial into the woman's hand. It was the Status Thief. Shakti slipped it into her breast pocket as though she understood that would explain everything before she headed toward the casino.

"She's a good person."

"Yes, one of the people I respect."

Lyu led the way out of the pool area, responding with a reverent voice as Syr smiled. Thanks to Shakti, *Ganesha Familia* was shorthanded, and they were able to slip through the perimeter. Hearing about what had happened in the Grand Casino, guests from the other casinos noisily flooded the elliptical plaza. While the guests glanced at the enormous fountain in the center of the plaza, Lyu, Syr, and Anna escaped the crowded Casino Strip. As they turned in to the complex back alleys of the Shopping District, a horse-drawn carriage came into view.

Lyu and Syr had hired it beforehand to wait in this alley.

"Take this carriage."

"Eh? B-but..."

"It will go to where your mother and father are. Everything will be all right after this."

Lyu and Syr stopped in front of the carriage with a waiting animal person driver, indicating Anna should leave by herself. If she returned to her parents now and changed her clothes, no one would know she had been bought by the owner. The adventurers who had kidnapped her had also been threatened into silence. She could return to being a normal city girl.

Opening the carriage's door, Anna clutched her chest, her eyes wavering. As if finally deciding something, she turned and leaned toward Lyu.

"Excuse me! I understand very well that you have a wife who you love! And that what I'm about to say might be troubling! However, even so, you put your life on the line to save me, and I..."

Lyu started blinking and Syr looked puzzled.

Anna gazed passionately at Lyu, like a *maiden in love*. Suddenly, Lyu felt her cheek twitching slightly.

The damp-eyed girl in front of her had misunderstood. It was a grave misconception.

"I lov—"

"Please wait."

"Eh?"

"You've misunderstood."

Lyu removed her eye patch, recognizing that she was suppressing extraordinarily strong feelings as she spoke. She ran her hands through her hair, mussing the clean look she wore for the disguise. Returning to her normal hairstyle.

"I'm a woman, just like you," she said with a hint of irony as her normal hairstyle returned.

Dumbstruck, Anna froze for an instant. Time seemed to stop before Anna let out a loud shout.

"Eeeeeeeeeeeeh~~~~~~?!"

Her pitiful wail echoed through the alley. The knight who had risked life and limb to come to her aid was in reality a beauty in men's clothes, a grown woman like her. The romantic tale that had set her heart aflutter crumbled pitifully. In a stupor, half in tears, Anna finally shuffled into the carriage, so unsteadily that they were a bit worried about her.

The wheels started spinning as the horse neighed, and the carriage passed the pair, carrying a heartbroken young girl.

"..."

"Eh-heh-heh..."

As the dry night breeze blew through the alley, Lyu pursed her lips. Next to her, Syr turned away, covering her mouth with both hands as her shoulders shook. Lyu bitterly watched the girl whose plan it was in the first place to have her cross-dress struggle to contain her laughter.

"There was a big mess at the casino! The aristocrats won't shut up about it!"

"Somehow the safe was busted up, and a huge amount of money was stolen, I hear!"

A crowd was forming on South Main Street in front of the arched gate entrance to the Casino Strip. The adventurers and normal people who were in the Shopping District noticed the hubbub and came to see what was happening. Information spread far and wide, the rumors getting more elaborate and exaggerated as they were passed along. Lyu stared out at the scene from the corner of a shady alleyway, watching as red and blue, yellow, and multicolor magic-stone lamps lit the Shopping District.

Syr was not with her anymore. She had split off, saying she was going to return the clothes she had borrowed. Going home in a ball gown would obviously attract attention, so she had headed to the shop of the merchant who let her borrow it. Syr had insisted Lyu should just wait, since it was so close by, then headed off to give the elf a chance to cool down after the fight.

"…"

Hidden in the shadows, she watched the developments unfolding at the casino. She looked on as countless Guild members filed inside—surely in order to take care of Ted and his underlings. At this point, even without any interference from her, things would be taken care of. Thinking that, Lyu relaxed her shoulders.

That's…Cranell.

She saw staff members and *Ganesha Familia* tossing Bell, Mord, Scott, and Guile out of the Casino Strip by. Thrown to the ground, Mord's group immediately grabbed Bell. They clutched his collar and shook him as he desperately apologized over and over. The scene drew the interest of the onlookers, who watched closely.

I caused problems for them, too…

Lyu felt bad for drawing them into her circumstances. As Mord and his friends started uncharacteristically weeping, she saw Bell repeatedly lowering his head.

At that instant, almost like a rabbit sensing someone's gaze, Bell turned around toward her. They were both startled as their eyes met. Watching his surroundings, Bell moved to the alley where Lyu was waiting carefully so as to avoid the notice of any onlookers.

"Miss Lyu! You're safe."

"Yes, thanks to your help. Are you guys okay?"

"We are fine. But, um…Miss Lyu, after that…"

"It's all over. The goal we came here for has been safely accomplished."

Bell did not really understand why they had infiltrated the casino, but he did not push any further. He smiled in relief, only saying, "That's good."

"Thank you for lending me a hand, Mr. Cranell. It helped. Also, for getting you wrapped up in this…I'm sorry."

"I-it's fine. You two are always helping me…"

"And I even caused problems for them."

"Mord and them are…well…Ah-ha-ha."

He looked over at the trio, who were still weeping. He instinctively feigned laughter, and then as if noticing something, he nervously asked Lyu a question.

"Umm, Miss Lyu? Did something happen? You seem a bit...different from normal..."

As Bell's words faded to a mumble, Lyu watched him with mild surprise. She would not call it brooding, but she certainly was thinking about several things.

"You are really good-looking, so it isn't surprising that you would be popular with women."

—A little while ago, Syr had said that. Lyu sighed as the girl finally controlled her laughter.

"...I get it already. I knew from the start that I don't have the sort of charm that you do."

"It's not like that."

Syr had smiled weakly in apology for having too much fun with Lyu, possibly because of Lyu's dark scowl. In the end, Anna's misunderstanding bothered her.

She had no intention of calling herself a maiden. She had the bluntness characteristic of the inflexible elves, and she was in the habit of standing tall and being exceedingly precise in every little move. She recognized she was the antithesis of the cuteness that captivated Bell when he saw Syr in her gown in the casino.

However, she was unwilling to accept being mistaken for a man. She had been so bothered about it that the boy had noticed it on her face.

Lyu stood still in silence for a little while. Her hand clutched her small bosom over her formal outfit. She finally spoke up without realizing it.

"Mr. Cranell...I'm not very feminine, am I?"

Lyu was shocked as she realized what she had said. Peering over at her, Bell blinked several times.

—*What am I saying? Am I losing my mind?*

She felt heat welling up in her cheeks in an instant. Embarrassed by her question, Lyu anxiously tried to correct herself.

"Mr. Cranell, just forg—"

"Hmm, Miss Lyu, you're..."

However, Bell was faster to respond.

"...strong, amazing, so good-looking that it makes a guy like me seem pathetic. But..."

Bell falteringly chose his words as Lyu stopped moving.

"You're also kind, polite, always holding your head high...and, umm...Miss Syr was definitely cute, but I—I...I also want to see what you look like in a gown someday..."

Her sky-blue eyes opened wide.

"...When I try to imagine it, I think you would look very pretty."

Bell's ears turned red as his words drifted into mumbles. Lyu's cheeks were burning with a different kind of warmth from before. Her heartbeat fluttered in her breast.

Bell did not notice her odd behavior as he struggled to put together unfamiliar words of praise. His white hair shifting, he kept glancing from side to side. Seeing the boy's silly movements, Lyu calmed down, and her eyes narrowed slightly as she asked in surprise:

"Do you always say things like that to women?"

"Eh?! O-of course not! It's just that my gramps used to say that if I wanted to cheer a woman up, then I should praise her until she smiles!! Ah, but what I said wasn't just flattery! I meant it—Uwaaaaaa...!"

Desperately trying to explain himself, he had revealed his true feelings and dug his grave deeper. Bell clutched his head as he writhed in embarrassment.

Lyu quietly smiled. The small concerns bothering her disappeared. In their place, a warm, almost happy sort of feeling enveloped her. Like sunlight smiling through the trees in the middle of the woods.

Closing her eyes, Lyu silently whispered her thanks in her heart, yielding to that warmth for a little bit.

"Mr. Cranell."

"Y-yes."

She looked out at the main street as Bell raised his head. Lyu kept her gaze on the Shopping District as she spoke.

"Recently, I've been doing early morning training in the courtyard of the restaurant."

"...?"

"If it's convenient for you...would you like to join me?"

She did not look at him, but she felt a sense of surprise. After a little while, the boy responded with a seemingly happy voice.

"Yes, please let me!"

Lyu's lips cracked into a smile. As if moving on its own, her left hand clutched her breast stealthily again. Apologizing to her coworker, she decided to be a bit more honest about her own feelings. At that thought, her heart calmed somewhat.

"Um, that is, I might not be able to come every day, though..."

"Of course. Just come when you have free time," she said as she continued to look out at the Shopping District.

Under the innumerable lights, in one corner of a back alley that faced a brilliant night street, an elf and a young man exchanged promises.

The dark sky had blue tinges to it as it gradually lightened. Early morning. The eastern sky signaled the beginning of a new day.

"In the end, what happened to that one casino, meow?" Ahnya asked as she yawned.

In the kitchen of the restaurant The Benevolent Mistress, Syr was working to make lunch, peeling a fruit as she answered.

"The Grand Casino is going on just as it was before. All that has changed is the owner. The management is continuing from there, they said."

"Santorio Vega is pretty brazen..."

"Well, that city isn't going to be discouraged by something like that, meow."

Having just changed into the tavern's uniform, Runoa and Chloe joined the conversation. It appeared that the real Terry Cervantes who had been sent from Santorio Vega somehow died in an unfortunate accident shortly before arriving. Ted was there and happened to witness it.

He had successfully assumed Terry's identity and become the

owner himself. He managed to pull it off thanks to his connections in the city from the Dark Age.

He paid exorbitant bribes to investigators from Santorio Vega to scrape by, and he used his bodyguards to secretly take care of people who knew the real Terry Cervantes and any troublemakers who could not be persuaded gently.

Now that the Status Thief had revealed his true identity, Ted answered everything during the Guild's questioning. Santorio Vega obviously cut him loose, happy to push the narrative that they were blameless for what had happened. In short, Ted took the fall for everything.

Still quivering in fear from *something* that happened that night, he was currently locked away in one of the Guild's solitary cells. Syr and the rest did not know what kind of political deal had been struck with the Guild, but the owner had been replaced, and El Dorado Resort returned to the same gambling paradise it was before. The women of Ted's menagerie were apparently given hefty reparations and sent back to their homelands.

"Seems like *Ganesha Familia* is getting all the credit for it, but is that okay with you two?"

"It's not like Lyu was looking for thanks when she went to help."

"Mya-ha-ha, the ally of justice's identity can't be exposed, meow."

As far as the world was concerned, the trail of the elf and human disguising themselves as the count and countess had gone cold.

The small number of adventurers and gods who knew their true identities kept their mouths shut, and it turned into a hot topic of discussion among the aristocrats and the wealthy who knew nothing. As a result, the reports from people who saw them at the time were wildly inconsistent: a band of robbers aiming for the casino's vault, operatives hired by the Guild working behind the scenes, envoys of justice who had returned, etc.…It ended up all being rumors without a bit of truth to them. *Ganesha Familia* stopped their investigation, unable to determine who the perpetrator was. Syr smiled uncomfortably as Runoa and Chloe closed in, getting worked up.

"That aside, I wanted to go see what sort of villains tried to take our names, meow. I wanted to use my patented sticky torture on them to extract payment for borrowing my name without permission, meow."

"There it is. Your methods are always so sleazy, you vulgar cat."

"I don't want to hear that from a muscle-brained human who tries to solve everything with force, meow."

"“Ah?”"

"That reminds me, what happened to that family, meow? Did the daughter return, meow?"

Ignoring the former bounty hunter and former assassin who were staring at each other, foreheads butting, Ahnya looked as if she had just remembered something.

"Yes, the Kreizes are—"

As Syr was about to answer, a wild uproar came from inside the tavern.

"Syr?! Lyu knocked the Little Rookie into the air again, meow!"

"She went too far...Wait—with her level, meow?!"

"Argh, Lyu!"

As her coworkers called out, Syr puffed out her cheeks in a pout as she ran over. The elf and boy had training sessions in the courtyard of the tavern from time to time. Ahnya, Chloe, and Runoa shrugged and laughed before following after her.

"What are you idiot girls doing, abandoning your jobs?!"

The dwarf proprietress's loud voice boomed as The Benevolent Mistress was plunged into chaos early that day.

7

"Oh, you are...it's been a while. Doing all right?"

In a dark, dismal tavern, a human was lightly lifting a mug of cheap ale to his mouth in one of the corners of the establishment.

"The Benevolent Mistress...? Ahh, you really went? Well, how did it turn out?"

The surrounding patrons' voices were low, coarse, and in a good mood. Amid the loud songs and laughter of men with their arms tossed over each other's shoulders, he grinned.

"You were thrown out the door?—Bah-ha-ha-ha! That's what I told you, didn't I? If you do something stupid, you'll get beat up!"

The man grabbed his stomach as he guffawed. As if taking pity on his companion, he slid the plate of bacon he was eating over to the other seat.

"So what did you do?...What, you try to do something to cute little Syr? You dumbass! That girl is the scariest one in that shop! The others don't have anything on her!"

The man downed his ale in good spirits.

"When I did it, it was that dwarf mistress who tossed me out. All the way into the middle of the street. I barely missed getting run over by a horse cart, you know?"

Reflecting on how dangerous it had been, the man let his voice falter. Almost as though the other guests seeking ale were sympathizing with him, the clamor went up a level.

"Hm? This wound? No, you've got it all wrong. I didn't get this from the women at that bar. This was...a scratch from my wife and my daughter. I really pissed them off."

Tracing the fresh wound left on his face, he laughed in embarrassment. Smelling faintly of liquor, his cheeks reddened and his eyes narrowed.

"I was an idiot and lost my only daughter. But she helped me, at that bar...that earnest, fastidious, charming elf did."

He laughed a bit, as though saying that she really was a stupid elf—though it was ironic coming from a man who put himself down.

"She cleaned up after an idiot like me, she got my home and my daughter back for me...and I was so ashamed I swore in front of my family that I would never gamble again, that I'd become an honest man."

Someone else laughed, rubbing his finger under his nose as he interrupted. "But..."

"...About that, just a little bit of alcohol hidden away from the girls is okay, right?"

He playfully laughed, spending a little bit of the day's earnings on a small reward for himself.

"—Father! Argh, I can't believe you're d-drinking in a place like this!"

"A-Anna?"

At that point, the bar's door had burst open. A flaxen-haired beauty stepped onto the stage, and some of the guests got excited. The man's lips twitched.

"You promised you wouldn't drink anymore!"

"Aah, that's not it Anna! Just one glass, it was really just a single glass! It was just one little bit of fun to end the month! Please let me have this!"

"I'm telling Mother! If Miss Lyu and the others found out, I'd be embarrassed, too!"

In an instant, the man who had been such a pitiful father stood up from his seat as his daughter dragged him by the arm. He turned his eyes to the seat across from him, smiling bitterly as the guests around him jeered and whistled.

"A bit of advice from someone with a few more years of experience: Keep bad things in moderation. And also, if you are ever unfortunate enough to get wrapped up in something...then try going to The Benevolent Mistress.

"But only when you're desperate and there's nothing else you can do. A fairy might help you out."

The man said that with a smile, and then his gorgeous daughter dragged him out of the bar.

THAT IS A BENEVOLENT TAVERN

~ Girl Meets Girls ~

1

"A contract? Again?"

Runoa Faust was a bounty hunter. Ever since the head god of the familia she belonged to had left this realm, she had traveled from place to place, changing factions as she went, getting contract requests every day. Hunting bounties was how she covered her traveling expenses.

At the moment, the wandering girl found herself in the Labyrinth City, Orario.

Because of her strength, she was known as Black Fist in the underworld here.

"Gale Wind's killing spree wiped out the last of the Evils. Isn't the power struggle already over?"

She was in a tavern on the outskirts of the outskirts. Buried in a back alley, down a flight of stairs, several demi-humans were having secretive conversations. When she took contracts, she always used this bar.

"Gale Wind is the target this time."

Runoa wore a scarf to cover the bottom half of her face. Across from her was a human merchant. Catching wind of her real strength, he had ignored the other people in the bar and brought the contract to her. Runoa's clientele tended to bring unwelcome favors.

"I heard Gale Wind kicked the bucket in the cross fire from that."

"Gale Wind is still alive, and she left us a clue in the end. Right after the Evils' hideout was destroyed, someone saw a bloodstained elf running away."

A detailed likeness was lying on the tabletop. The parchment showed the instant the elf ran past, a side view of a haggard face through broken pieces of a mask. Sunken sky-blue eyes, beautiful golden hair—an elf woman.

"My men investigated, and we know where she fled to as well. She's at The Benevolent Mistress."

Saying this, the merchant put a small bag with the advance payment on the table.

"One of the men under my protection was injured during Gale Wind's most recent spree. Not only that, she might have found out that our Bruno Corporation was connected to the Evils. Before that gets out, erase her."

He got up without waiting for a reply, letting his words and the gold speak for themselves. After the client left the bar, Runoa took a deep breath.

"...Well, I said I'll take care of anyone as long as I get my reward, but..."

Runoa had gotten this far on brute strength alone. She had captured bounty after bounty in order to make an easy livelihood. But she was gradually getting tired.

"Orario's adventurers are a little too strong..."

The adventurers in the Labyrinth City got an order of magnitude stronger once you crossed a certain line. Even for Runoa's *almost* one hundred percent success rate on jobs, second-tier adventurers and above were inevitably difficult fights. First-tier adventurers were an instant no. Orario was a hive of superhuman monsters, sunup to sundown and beyond, fighting every day. It was a negative feedback loop where she crushed her targets, raising her reputation, leading to more crazy jobs coming her way. Her nerves were wearing down more and more with each passing day. Even the mead that she had liked so much at this bar had lost its flavor.

"Argh. I'm already tired. I just want to be able to settle down and find someone to take care of me. I could lie around a small house all day, and he doesn't have to be attractive..."

Runoa Faust. Seventeen years old.

She grumbled like someone twice her age as she looked up at the ceiling.

"Maybe I should quit being a bounty hunter…?"

"Another contract? How many is that this month?"

Chloe Lolo was an assassin.

She had belonged to a certain crime familia, and after getting sick of the endless stream of compulsory jobs, she had completed the unreasonable task set by the head god and been allowed to leave. As she traveled, she earned her living as an assassin.

Currently, the stray cat found herself in the place known as the Center of the World, Orario. Due to the success rate of her assassinations, her name spread in the underworld under the alias Black Cat.

"Well, if you prepare a proportionate reward, I'll do the job, but…"

Wearing a hood, Chloe was in a belfry that had been abandoned years ago. The long-silent bell hung from the ceiling as tranquil moonlight poured through the arch. It was one of the places she used for meetings when she took contracts.

"Ah, of course. The target this time is Gale Wind."

The man standing before Chloe was a dwarf merchant. He seemingly had many enemies, and he was also greedy. Sensing opportunities for money, he was a business connection who gathered contracts for her.

"Hmm, Gale Wind…is still alive?"

"Yeah. If you take the job I'll give you the details. It's a first-class wanted person this time."

He handed over a single wanted poster. Drawn on it was a masked adventurer wearing a deep hood. The sum written above the likeness was 80,000,000 valis.

"A bounty worth that much is unheard of. We got it before anyone else. The money'll be an even split—"

"Forty million in advance. And I'll take seventy percent of the reward," she cut in, shutting down his proposal.

"W-wait. Even for you…it should at least be sixty-forty…" he responded, suddenly flustered.

"No. You can say she's gotten weaker, but this is the monster who destroyed the Evils single-handedly…Taking out someone like her…if I don't get at least that much, it isn't worth it." Chloe stubbornly stood her ground.

The hood she wore fluttered in the night breeze. It was deep enough to cover her eyes, with two little peaks from her cat ears befitting the name Black Cat. The crescent moon illuminated the small movements of her lips.

"I can just do it myself, you know? I could always drag the information out of you."

"O-okay, I got it…we'll split it how you said."

The dwarf gulped and assented, disinclined to argue with an assassin who specialized in torture. He handed over the parchment with information about Gale Wind and left the belfry as if running for his life.

"…Easy, meow."

Once she was alone, Chloe's tone of voice changed, and she heaved a heavy sigh.

"That killjoy had a no backbone, not tasty at all, meow…Bringing back the contract sooner would be better, meow."

Chloe had gotten here on just her assassination ability.

Business was business, so she put on a facade that could not be looked down on and threw herself into the business of the night. But she was increasingly tired.

"Assassination here just doesn't pay off, meow. All the money I work to earn ends up going to pay for the preparations for the next job, meow."

As far as Chloe and her *almost* one hundred percent success rate were concerned, Orario's adventurers were too strong. The elaborate preparations required to assassinate them ate up all the rewards. Once, she had gotten lucky and taken out a second-tier adventurer. After that, the jobs were all challenges, and by the time she had painstakingly set up a gravestone, people were coming with new coffins for her to fill. Her painstakingly groomed tail that she took so much pride in was whipping up a storm.

"Ahhh. I want to live an elegant life with a handsome boy waiting on me already, meow. I want a slice of heaven where he pats my tummy and butt and makes my heart race until I've had my fill, meow."

Chloe Lolo. Sixteen years old.

Secretly filled with desire, the young catgirl whispered as she looked up at the moon. "Maybe I should quit the assassination business, meow…"

2

Rain was falling.

It was a cold rain. It washed everything away. The specks of blood dropping to the stone pavement mixed with the drops, melted, and disappeared.

"…"

Lyu walked by herself, dragging her wounded body through the empty back alley.

She did it.

She had finished it.

She had gotten her revenge.

She had destroyed them all: the familia that had stolen her comrades and all those who supported it.

However, that retribution would not bring back what she had lost. It only brought an empty feeling.

"…Where am I…?"

Her field of vision, which had been crimson tinted, now turned gray.

Her friends' smiles, their final pained expressions—she could not remember any of it anymore. The tears that had poured from her eyes and the lamentations that had rushed from her lips had disappeared somewhere along the line.

She knew she had become empty.

The fury that had kept her moving had turned to a boundless darkness coiling around her heart. And in that never-ending darkness, Lyu was no longer attached to life.

As though condemning her, the cold rain from heaven stole her warmth. As though the gods had willed it. The foolish death of an elf who had strayed from her path.

Her body was so covered in blood there was no longer any telling what was hers and what was her enemies'. Wheezing as massive pain racked her heavily injured body, Lyu tried to move limbs suffering from unprecedented fatigue, and she collapsed like a puppet whose strings had been cut. She fell into a puddle, dirtying her body with splashes of mud. She began to freeze.

...Unsightly.

It was a cold night. She lay in a circle of dim light born of a used-up magic-stone lamp. This was where Lyu died. No one to care for her, in some dark, dirty back alley. A fitting end for a foolish fairy.

Goddess Astrea...Alizé.

The goddess's sweet smile flashed in her mind. Her affectionate words rang in her ears.

She wanted to hear the voice of her friend who was already gone and at peace one last time. Embracing those conflicting emotions, Lyu waited for her death, gradually closing her eyes.

"—You okay?"

However.

As Lyu's consciousness slid into the dark abyss, someone reached out a hand.

"...?"

She could faintly see a girl in front of her as she opened her eyes. Bluish-silver hair shifted under the poncho she was wearing. The girl's voice resembled the gentle call of the chief goddess, and also her departed friend. The girl kneeled down and kindly grasped Lyu's blood- and grime-covered right hand.

...aaah.

My hand that refused the touch of other people—accepted her hand.

Soft.

Warm.

Kind.

Wrapped in warmth, something spilled from Lyu's dried up eyes.

—*"It's not time for you to come yet."*

She thought she could hear her old friend's voice, and her consciousness completely faded.

The instant she realized the dream had ended...

Lyu's eyes opened.

"—!"

Her eyelids opened wide. She was looking at a wooden ceiling. The feeling of sheets and a blanket wrapped around her body indicated she had slept in a bed. What she was seeing was not a memory but an actual wooden room. Morning sunlight shone through a window.

"This is—Gah!"

As she sluggishly tried to sit up, her upper body immediately collapsed.

Lyu was assaulted by a wave of pain and weariness. As she fell back into the blanket, she noticed the bandages wrapped around her arms. Someone had given her medical treatment. Perplexed by the unknown room, and the smell wafting through the air, she heard light footsteps as a girl opened the door and came in.

"Ah, you woke up. Great."

"...You are..."

"Don't try to do too much, okay? You were really badly hurt."

The newcomer holding bandages and a washcloth was the same platinum-haired girl Lyu had seen in the back alley. She was wearing some kind of shop's uniform, just like in Lyu's memories. It was clear she had carried Lyu to this room and cared for her.

"You were asleep for three days. It's good you were able to wake up."

"Three days..."

Hearing that number, Lyu was not particularly surprised. Her only thought was:

I'm still alive. That was all.

"I'm Syr Flover."

As Lyu blankly looked ahead, the girl, Syr, introduced herself. She was cute. An affable smile floated across her face as if to put Lyu at ease, speaking to her kindness. She was the exact opposite of Lyu, who tended to be especially frank in her responses.

Someone who could just naturally get people to smile; "girl next door" was a perfect descriptor.

"This is a small building at the tavern that I work at. After I found you collapsed in the alley, I had you carried here—"

"Why?"

"Eh?"

Interrupting the girl, Lyu asked. Thoughts of regret and despair mixed together.

"Why did you help me?"

She had lost everything. Having killed her bitter enemy, she had no more reason to cling to life. The only thing left for her was emptiness. She could not find another reason to live on. Knowing just how empty her eyes were, Lyu looked back at the girl.

"Let's see..." Syr looked as though she was concerned about Lyu, smiling as she lowered her eyebrows. "I couldn't just leave someone so wounded in the rain."

"..."

It was an incredibly straightforward response. If Lyu were in her position, she would definitely have done the same.

Would she still be able to say that if she knew who I was?

Lyu was the Gale Wind. The most wanted person in Orario, who had brought chaos to the city.

"Were you not…suspicious of someone collapsed in a place like that?"

"At the moment, Orario is dangerous no matter what. And also, I'm used to people with special circumstances."

…Used to? People with special circumstances?

Doubtful, Lyu shifted her gaze back to Syr as she set the medical supplies on a shelf and knelt on the floor, looking up at her.

"Miss Elf, what's your name?"

"…And once you know, what will you do?"

"I'd like to call you by it."

When Syr responded so easily, Lyu's voice caught in her throat.

This is difficult. Her manner is strange. Who is this girl?

She did not have the willpower to live; she should have had eyes as empty as someone already dead. Nevertheless, as Syr kindly approached her, Lyu was confused.

She tried to turn away, attempting to reject the girl's innocent, sunny goodwill. However…

…She's the second person…

Lyu had not knocked her hand away. The first person had been the leader of *Astrea Familia*, her old friend Alizé Rovel, the one who invited her to join the familia. She had been the first and last person until this point. When people she had just met tried to shake her hand, Lyu instinctually batted them away.

However, that rainy day, in a dark back alley, the girl had grasped Lyu's hand.

The elf's hand that was so deeply stained in darkness had also not rejected Syr's hand.

She doesn't resemble Alizé at all. So why…?

She looked at Syr's smile and her hand. Unsure and with nowhere else to look, Lyu finally opened her mouth.

"Lyu…Lyu Leon."

"Lyu…That's a nice name." Hearing it, a smile bloomed on Syr's face like a flower.

Lyu's gaze fled to the blanket covering her. Syr and her joyful expression were definitely hard to deal with.

© NIRITSU

"*Cough!* Aaaanyway…" Faking a cough, she began:

"Lyuuuuu will…feeeeel…beeeeetter. Feeeeel better!" She started spinning her finger in front of Lyu's eyes and nose.

"…"

"Lyuuuuuuu wiiiiiiiiiill smile!"

Her finger kept moving. Lyu froze up like a statue.

What is this?

Some kind of ritual?

Is this a psychological attack?

"Yay!"

"?"

She pressed Lyu's nose for the finishing blow.

"It's a good-luck charm to make you feel better. I do it for the kids I know all the time, you know?"

Saying that, Syr smiled as though she had finished a hard task.

Unable to intercept it, Lyu again froze.

"…H-huh? You didn't start smiling? That's strange…"

Syr looked genuinely confused as she watched Lyu stay frozen. When Lyu's head finally started moving, she glared with half-closed eyes as if to say, *What are you doing? That's rude.*

Syr awkwardly forced a laugh. She did not notice Lyu's sullen look.

Lyu's eyes, which had been empty just a minute ago, started to cloud with emotion after her back-and-forth with the girl.

"That bed-ridden elf up yet?"

Just then, another person entered the room: a female dwarf with a good physique. She was tall for a dwarf, taller even than Lyu. The word *giant* fit her perfectly, and her earth-colored ponytail made a strong impression. Without saying a word, one could tell she had a hearty disposition.

"Yes, Mama. It seems her name is Lyu Leon. Lyu, this person is mistress of the place where I work. Her name is Mia."

Mia…?

As Syr stood up, the word "Mia" triggered a reaction in Lyu. A certain piece of information crossed her mind, but she shook her head immediately, dismissing it.

"Jeez, more hassles when I'm already short on staff. And it's not a stray dog or a stray cat you go picking up, but a pain-in-the-ass elf."

"But, Mama Mia, you let me, didn't you?"

As Mia's grumbles mixed with sighs, Syr smiled back.

Lyu knit her eyebrows. Mia talked like a dwarf who naturally did not get along well with elves. The mistress looked down at her.

"I saw the clothes and gear that she took off you…You're Gale Wind, aren't you?"

At that, Lyu's expression immediately changed. Her eyes sharpened to a piercing gaze. Hearing the name Gale Wind, Syr looked surprised.

"And if I am, what will you do? Hand me over to the Guild?"

Lyu knew that a wanted person like her was deemed dangerous. It was fair to say she had already abandoned herself. As Lyu confronted her, Mia snorted at the inanity of it all.

"Why would I need to do something annoying like that, idiot?"

"Wh—"

"When you can move again, then do whatever you want. You just have to pay a reasonable price for the three days you've stayed here."

Lyu looked stunned at her unthinkable response.

"Lyu? If it's convenient for you, why don't you stay here for a little while? If you stay at this tavern, you'll be safe. At least until the excitement has calmed down a bit."

What is this girl saying? It would be normal to be scared of a top-tier wanted person, or at least be excited by the opportunity to turn them in for money. Even if this is a trap, it would be pointless to trick me like this, though, since I can't resist anyway.

Lyu was confused by the fact that these two were entirely unconcerned about her identity. Her heart was in disarray.

"Mama Mia is reaaally strong. She can definitely protect you, Lyu. And I want to know more about you. So—"

Don't get any closer.

And stop looking at me with that smile.

Don't stick out your hand with a smile that reminds me of Alizé.

Lyu's throat quivered, unable to endure the anguish oozing inside her heart.

"I—I…!"

Without realizing it, she shouted as though trying to shake off her confusion.

"I…I already have nothing left—comrades, a place to return to…I did something incredibly foolish, and I should have died then." Her fingers dug into the blanket, and all the thoughts that were stored up in her heart spilled out in repentence.

"Lyu…" Seeing Lyu's distress, a sad, lonely expression appeared on Syr's face.

"Arrrgh! No way, no way. This is what you get from elves. High-strung and obstinate—it's annoying." Mia responded bluntly, paying no heed to Lyu's pained expression.

"Your life would have ended if she didn't do anything. You should at least think of it as good luck. And what is that crap you're saying? When did elves become so impolite they can't even say thanks to the person who saved their life?"

"Tch! Like a boorish dwarf could understand!"

Lyu forgot her pain in her indignation. She had become more flexible after entering *Astrea Familia*, but the elf's stubborn side was exposed here.

"My reason for living is already gone!"

As Lyu forcefully said that—*gurgle*. A cute sound rang out from her torso.

"…"

"…"

"…"

Lyu froze, Syr stared in puzzlement, and Mia was in shock. Recognizing that her stomach had growled while she was talking, the proud elf turned bright red as she flailed in embarrassment.

"Looks like your body still wants to live, though."

"Gah…!"

A huge disgrace. Thinking back on it, given her total exhaustion followed by three straight days of sleep, it was natural her body would want nutrients. Lyu had not felt this embarrassed in years. Spurred on by Syr's stifled laughter, her slender ears got hotter. As she looked down, she resented her physiological response.

"Mama Mia."

"Hm?"

Syr winked at Mia as though plotting something. Lyu was too busy wallowing in shame to notice.

Mia looked dubious, but Syr smiled suggestively in return.

"No way around it. Ignoring a hungry person will hurt the tavern's reputation. Come on, eat some food."

"W-wait a minute! I didn't say anything about wanting to eat—!" Lyu did not know when to give up. Mia did not let her finish her refusal, glaring as she grabbed the elf's head in a vise grip.

"?!"

"Your babbling is annoying. Listen to what people say, you stubborn elf."

".........?!"

Mia's large hand squeezed her head tightly, as if squashing a fruit. Still injured, Lyu could not evade it. She could not even react. More than anything, she could not escape the restraint at all. A trickle of sweat formed on the back of her head as the giant dwarf single-handedly restrained her. In that instant, Lyu understood the difference in strength between the two of them.

"Get changed and come get some food."

"Guh—"

Finally releasing Lyu, Mia turned around and lumbered out of the room. Breathing heavily, Lyu wiped away sweat as Syr whispered in her ear.

"Mama Mia is reeeeally scary when she gets mad. I think it would be better to come," Syr said with a cheerful smile.

Lyu looked back with frustration. She belatedly began to realize that she had been dropped into an outrageous place.

The reluctant elf was brought to the dining hall, a room not quite large enough to be called spacious. It was deserted; just the three of them were there. Mia disappeared for a little while into what was apparently the kitchen and returned carrying a plate with steam rising off it. It was a risotto with root vegetables of various colors and carefully boiled, finely cut chicken meat.

"There. Eat it before it's cold."

"Mama Mia's food is super-delicious."

"…"

She did not have the option to say no. She could imagine that vise grip on her head if she imprudently refused again. With a slightly reproachful glare at being forced to sit at the dinner table, Lyu picked up the spoon in resignation. She scooped up a little bit of the rice and vegetables and brought it to her lips.

"…"

First, the pleasant flavor of the broth-soaked rice spread through her mouth. Next was the flavor of the vegetables. They melted into the mellow rice and warmed the inside of her mouth. At the same time, the chicken meat split apart and seemed to melt on top of her tongue. The ingredients' natural flavors mixed together and supported each other. Lyu looked down at the risotto as a rich scent wafted up from the plate.

"…The flavor is strong. I prefer it simpler."

"That so?"

"Dwarf cooking is too rough. Skillful elf cooking is more refined."

"That's too bad."

Mia ignored Lyu's disinterested complaints, as though she did not care. Standing to the side, Syr watched over the graceful elf. Lyu listed multiple broad complaints, but finally, her cheeks lightly flushed, she whispered in wonder.

"But…it's warm and delicious."

Mia's mouth curved into a bold grin. Syr smiled broadly. Like a snowfield under the spring sun, Lyu's stiff cheeks finally softened. The dwarf mistress suddenly spoke up.

"'*Eat delicious food.*' That's a fine purpose to have in life, a reason to keep living."

The overly earnest Lyu, her body warmed by the food and the

tranquil flavor still on her tongue, mistook what Mia said for a wise proverb.

She's right; the reason people go on living might just be something like that.

Lyu picked up her spoon and ate another bite of risotto. And another. And another. Before long the plate was empty.

"Ho-ho! You ate all of it."

"...Thank you...very much."

As Syr took care of the plate, Lyu thanked them awkwardly. She looked down at her bandaged hands with an embarrassed expression on her face, her lips loosened ever so slightly, and she felt like a little bit of happiness had spread through her empty shell.

"So—*you ate it.*"

At that point...

Watching over Lyu from the side, Mia's tone of voice suddenly changed.

"That's the result of someone's labor, you know. Lots of valuable ingredients were put into it, too."

"...What are you saying?" Lyu's voice hardened again as she sensed a suspicious atmosphere.

"You didn't think that feast was free, did you? I let you eat some food, and I'll be sure to charge a price. I'll have you pay the bill in full." Mia grinned as she answered.

"The price...totals up to fifty million valis."

"Th-that's absurd!" Lyu slammed her hand on the table as she stood up forcefully, doubting her ears the moment she heard the price.

"Seems like you can't pay. Guess I've got no choice. I'll have you work here to pay off what you owe," Mia continued, unconcerned.

"Wh...!"

"It's perfect, since I've been low on staff."

She was lost for words as the dwarf mistress said that without any hesitation, as though she had planned it. Shocked, Lyu felt her voice rising.

"That's oppression—fraud!! Like I'd let you get away with an excuse like that...!"

Lyu would normally never lose her composure to this extent. Ordinarily, she would have instantly retaliated against an outrage like this, but she could not. Because Mia was stronger.

Her clenched fists trembled at the unreasonable humiliation she was suffering.

"This is Orario, you know? You never know what'll happen, aboveground or in the Dungeon."

Like a towering boulder, Mia did not waver in her arrogant demand. Lyu turned to Syr.

"In this tavern, whatever Mama Mia says is absolute~~."

This girl's just crying crocodile tears…!

As Lyu's face gradually twitched, Mia delivered the finisher.

"Syr is right. Here we go by my law. If I say black is white, then it's white."

The giant dwarf smiled viciously.

—Looking back on this later, Lyu would recognize this series of events was a pretext to cheer her up. Syr and Mia were desperately conspiring to get her to keep going. However, there was no way Lyu would understand that at the time.

—I've been had!

The elf was screaming in her mind.

"It's decided. I'll have you work as an employee at my tavern."

From that day forward, Lyu was forced to work at The Benevolent Mistress.

Eight thousand valis rent. That was the cost of the apartment Runoa was leasing.

"I took it in the end, but…should this be my last job?"

The location was in the city's northwest block, seventh district. It was a corner of Orario near the giant wall that encircled the city. The three-story apartment building got no sunlight thanks to the wall, and it was cold at night because the building was made of stone. Runoa had taken a liking to this property. Because of the location, no one came by. People living in the building were all poor or had something to hide, like Runoa.

And since the dwarf owner's stated policy was "As long as you pay your rent, I don't care," Runoa was grateful to not have anyone prying into her business unnecessarily. And best of all, it was quiet. The occasional person talking to themselves and ominous laughter coming from the room next door were a bit of an annoyance, though…

Bounty hunting was a profession where it was easy to make enemies, so she had not told anyone this address.

"If it's going to be my last, then I'll end with a win. Well…except this one is Gale Wind, though."

The single stone room had only a handful of furnishings, the bare minimum: crude wooden bed, magic-stone lamp, etc.

The only thing of note was her work outfit—the black gauntlets and battle clothes—and a handmade sandbag.

The wooden chair creaked as Runoa sat down, after turning on the magic-stone stove to make a pot of hot milk. She looked over the information sheet for her target.

"Other than the place she's hiding, there's nothing. Even if she always wore a mask to hide her identity, it's weird they don't even know her full name. Adventurers are supposed to be registered with the Guild, aren't they?"

The paper she had received from the corporation that supposedly had the profile of Gale Wind did not even have a description of the person.

Useless. Runoa grimaced.

"Dammit, Guild, don't publish worthless information…"

The Guild was covering for Gale Wind. She was the last living member of *Astrea Familia*, who had worked with them to maintain the peace and order of the city.

No, protecting her isn't quite right. Maybe a final mercy is a bit closer.

Gale Wind had lost herself in revenge, exacting retribution against all the merchants and adventurers who supported her enemies—even the Guild members who had worked with them—so they could not get away without punishing her. They had revoked her status as an adventurer and registered her on the blacklist. The organization had kept up appearances.

"It doesn't seem like there's any more information, though... Guess I have to check it out myself."

Once she decided, she jumped into action. That was Runoa Faust, bounty hunter. Grabbing the scarf she always wore, she stood up. Her destination was the tavern The Benevolent Mistress, where Gale Wind had been taken. Quickly finishing her preparations, she opened the door and headed for that bar.

"*Astrea Familia*...That faction's rank was B. Eleven members, all of them second-tier adventurers. They reached the forty-first floor, cleared twenty-one floor bosses...Mrrow, the more I read, the more monstrous she looks."

Lying on a bed in her underwear, Chloe murmured. Her single stone room had an extravagantly plush carpet, a bed with a canopy on it, a chandelier-style magic-stone lamp, and magic-stone fireplace, everything heavily customized in order to be more luxurious. It was without a doubt a palace for Chloe alone, the epitome of bad taste and wasteful spending.

For the price, the room was perfect...other than that from time to time she could hear the dull sounds of something being struck in the room next door.

This was the secret address of the one feared in the underworld as Black Cat.

Propping her cheek up as she lay on the bed, her black cattail wriggling from her similarly colored lingerie, Chloe sighed as she looked down at the parchment.

"You can tell how tough she is just from the Guild's public information, meow. This familia caught a lot of the Evils."

The information sheet spread across her pillow was not about Gale Wind herself, but about the faction she belonged to—the no-longer-extant *Astrea Familia*.

"According to the Guild's public information, Gale Wind was a Level Four. But if you add in that she destroyed the final ally of the

Evils, *Rudra Familia*, by herself…then she is top class among Level Fours, no doubt, meow."

Ah, I don't want to kill her, Chloe thought as she lay facedown on the pillow.

Level Fours are hard to do, and if I'm not careful, I'll get killed in the cross fire.

Regret over jumping the gun welled up in her chest.

"…Oh well, meow. This is my last job anyway, meow. I'm getting a lot of money for this, and after I run away from here, I can live easy with lots of cute boys to take care of me, meow."

Chloe giggled evilly to herself as wicked ideas ran through her mind. Losing herself in wild daydreams for a little while, the catgirl rolled on her back and held her slender hand up to the light.

"Finishing off Gale Wind will be my crowning glory, meow."

She hopped to her feet and put on the tunic and robe that lay carelessly on the floor.

Facing someone truly strong head-on was suicide. Therefore, assassination—the ability to freely use poison, traps, and the like at the right time and right place to take someone out unaware. To do that, it was necessary to understand the target's habits and area of activity.

She was not going to be lazy about gathering information on her target. This was Chloe Lolo, assassin. Her target was the tavern The Benevolent Mistress, where Gale Wind had escaped. Wearing her hood for disguise, Chloe opened the door to her room.

""Uhn?""

As the two doors thudded closed at the same time, Chloe and Runoa saw each other. Both were dressed up like they were going out. Neighbors who had not met before today.

Who's that sick-looking human, meow?

Who's this degenerate catgirl?

They kept their opinions to themselves. Chloe snickered at the human who did not care about her appearance, and Runoa made a dubious face at the mysterious catgirl hiding her eyes.

"..."

"..."

Both silent, they locked their doors and proceeded down opposite hallways. They recognized each other as having guilty consciences and knew nothing good would come of interacting. Their backs to each other, they left the apartment building by different routes, but they were headed toward the exact same place.

"No..."

Lyu stood in front of the dresser murmuring in shock. A waitress was reflected in the mirror.

She was wearing a light green dress that went below her knees with a white apron wrapped around her body. Feared as Leon of the Gale Wind, Lyu felt incredibly out of place in a cutesy uniform like this. If her comrades in the lost familia were here now, they would burst out laughing, no doubt. Goddess Astrea would definitely be trying to hide giggles.

Her shining gold hair had even been dyed a light green color.

"It looks good on you, Lyu! You're super-cute! Just to be safe, I dyed your hair so that no one will recognize you as Miss Gale Wind."

While Lyu was shocked, Syr was enjoying herself, an affable tone in her voice. It was several days after that fateful day when they had decided she would work at the tavern. Lyu had finally gotten healthy again and was reborn as an employee of The Benevolent Mistress. Mostly because of Syr. By force.

Lyu found Syr's unreserved smile and praise unbearably detestable right now. She wanted to take off the white cap on her head and pummel it into the ground.

"Allll right, let's get right to work. Time to pay back that expensive meal, right?"

"Kuh."

Smirking, Syr warned her that unapproved movements would not be allowed. As a duty-bound elf, it was calamitous for Lyu. If she ran away without returning the favor to people who had made so much effort to heal her, not to mention fed her, the honor of her proud forest species would be sullied.

Because of that, even if she had been treated badly, Lyu's morals would not let her run away, no matter how much she wanted to do so. Even for the peculiar members of *Astrea Familia*, such a thing was unheard of.

"I'll introduce you to Ahnya and the others later, but first I'll teach you the job."

"Hey, what do you say when someone teaches you something?"

There was nowhere to run.

Lyu was pinned on either side by the smiling Syr and Mia with her arms crossed.

"Thank you…in advance…" Her voice quivered as she whispered, her cheeks turning bright red in embarrassment.

Thus began Lyu's daily struggle.

Everyone's first job at The Benevolent Mistress—was peeling.

"Newbie, can you peel vegetables, meow?"

"…Where I was before, it was usually catered."

"People always think it doesn't look that bad, meow. Here, if you just hold the knife like thi—"

"—Don't touch me!"

"Fugyah?!"

"Kyaah! Lyu knocked Ahnya into the vegetables!"

"What are you doing, you dumbass!!"

"Kuh!"

Thanks to her aversion toward being touched, she had knocked her coworker down—failure.

Her second job at The Benevolent Mistress involved going shopping.

"Okay, Lyu? When you're buying ingredients, give a cute smile. And it's fine to beg a bit."

"Give a cute smile…beg…"

"Yep, if you do that, they'll give you lower prices. It'll be okay; the old guys at the shop are nice! So good luck!"

"Understood…Shopkeeper."

"Oh, that uniform—The Benevolent Mistress, eh? What do you need today?"

"Those fruits. Please give me a discount."

"Eh?"

"I said discount, please."

"Um, that's…"

"Please do it quickly. Are you trying to insult me?"

"Y-yikes?! Help me—!"

"Lyu! That's not pleading, that's threatening! And cramping your face isn't smiling; you look like a hit man!!"

"Kuh!"

Banned from the greengrocer—failure.

The third job at The Benevolent Mistress was serving customers.

"…The menu."

"Oh, a new staff member? Quite the beauty, too! But kind of blunt."

"Kuh!"

The guests did not like her expression—failure.

And the jobs after that, too: failure, failure, and failure. A storm of disappointments.

"You're more useless than I thought…" Mia sighed heavily.

"Kuhhh…!"

When Mia called her out, Lyu endured the humiliation.

This is wrong. It's because I only just started. I'm just nervous because it's an unknown experience. Even refined adventurers make big mistakes in the face of the "Unknown."

Lyu was decidedly not useless, she reassured herself with a loud voice in her head.

…No, it was like this when I was with Alizé, wasn't it?

When she had joined *Astrea Familia*, Lyu had constantly made mistakes. At the time, she had caused problems for the chief goddess Astrea and her friend Alizé.

When I'm not used to things, I always make mistakes.

"At this rate, instead of paying back the food, you're just acquiring more debt."

"Kuhh..."

Ashamed, Lyu continued her trials.

Why is Gale Wind working as a waitress...?

Outside the window, the sun was setting in the blue sky. Going undercover as a customer at The Benevolent Mistress to gather information, Runoa was confused at the spectacle she saw. The elf was wearing a waitress uniform, interacting with customers and taking away plates with a gloomy face.

A wanted person who's even on the Guild's blacklist suddenly got a part-time job at a bar...No way, I don't understand at all...

The elf matched the description and likeness she had received from the corporation. Her hair seemed to have been dyed, but it was unmistakably the same person.

However, Gale Wind—who once sent tremors down the spine of all the villains in the city—had exchanged her bloodstained battle clothes and hood for a waitress uniform and white headpiece...

What is that look? I want to laugh, but I can't.

"...Hey, hey, waitress, is that elf employee new?"

"Yes, meow. So new that she needs to be watched constantly, meow. At the moment, I'm taking of her myself, meow!"

But you're messing up orders, too, you stupid cat.

Annoyed at the waitress's self-satisfaction when she had brought coffee instead of the black tea she had ordered, Runoa peeked over at Gale Wind again. She was moving around the tavern with a distinct lack of familiarity, and even writing down the orders from the patrons was a struggle. She was somehow managing with the gallant help of a blue-and-silver-haired girl.

A ruse to throw off trackers, or a trap...? But this looks too stupid.

While watching the ill-tempered elf from the side, she sipped her coffee. Looking around at the smiling women guests, she struggled to figure out how to handle the situation.

Why is Gale Wind doing chores at a bar, meow?

Under the same setting sun...

Chloe was pretending to be a messenger and sneaking glances through the back door of the store. The scene unfolding before her eyes shocked her. She watched as the elf was called to the back of the kitchen and scolded by the dwarf mistress.

"It seems pretty busy, but what's wrong with that elf girl?" She tried probing a bit while handing over a letter addressed to the tavern.

"Ahh, sorry. She just started...She messed up a bit, so she's getting some advice." The blue-and-silver-haired girl answered with a hint of a wry smile.

Chloe was confident that the elf was Gale Wind when she heard "just started"...but just like a certain bounty hunter, she could not shake her confusion.

Also, that dwarf...she's super-scary, meow. Don't want to make that frumpy woman mad...

Even from afar, she could recognize the dangerous potential of the mistress's anger.

Gale Wind was quietly nodding and putting up with the scolding, her expression like that of a monk in training who had endured several hours under a waterfall.

"Miss Courier...are you new? Are you that interested in our tavern?" The girl smiled sweetly as Chloe quickly confirmed Gale Wind and the layout of the bar.

"...Aaah, that was rude of me. As you guessed, I'm a provisional employee. Anyway, I've confirmed the letter has been delivered."

Acting normal, Chloe returned the smile and left via the back door. She jogged through a back alley where the sun did not reach.

"Whew, that was dangerous," she whispered to herself as she pulled down the brim of the hat she wore as a disguise. "I can't let my guard down in there, meow…The footsteps of the chefs in the kitchen were awfully quiet, it seemed…"

From my perspective, that platinum haired girl is dangerous, too.

This was Orario. People were trained to deal with wild hooligans, including adventurers, but…

"A bar that puts Gale Wind to work…that place might be bad news, meow?"

Making an odd face as she whispered, she wondered if she might have *hit the bull's-eye*—

"Ha-ha, no way."

The skilled assassin couldn't help but laugh away the absurd thought.

Yes, she foolishly laughed it off.

"Haaa, I'm tired, meow. Mama is rough with both people and cats, meow."

Ahnya complained as she and Lyu carried groceries.

No comment on the cat part, but she does use people roughly, Lyu agreed silently.

Several days had already passed since she had started working at The Benevolent Mistress. She had repeatedly messed up, but she was working as an obedient tavern employee.

"Ah, Lyu. Hold the basket properly! If the vegetables fall, Mama will yell at you again, meow!"

"…I think it's fine."

"Letting your guard down like that will cost you your life, meow! I've slipped countless times! I've been doing this longer than you, so you should listen to what I say, meow! Fufun!"

Falling down and holding a basket aren't related, though. Plus, you're awfully proud saying that.

After Syr, this Ahnya girl was the next person Lyu had gotten to know. She seemed cheerful and simple. An idiot…or at least lacking in some way. The way she kept trying to touch Lyu's hand, no matter how many times the elf countered by knocking her away, was good evidence.

She tried to give off an air of seniority and experience, but no matter how Lyu looked at it, she was still better…on paper. Objectively, maybe. By a slim margin.

"…At any rate…"

"?"

"You still look so gloomy, meow. Kind of…depressed, meow? It's concerning, meow…"

Lyu was at a loss for words as Ahnya spoke bluntly, placing the basket of vegetables on the table.

For better or worse, the thoughtless catgirl had no restraint. Recognizing she was right, Lyu could not respond. She had been made to work plenty at this tavern, but there was still a gaping *hole* in her heart. It would unintentionally reveal itself, and her expression would darken.

"…Sorry for making you worry."

Maybe Ahnya has been paying so much attention to me because she is worried about me. Thinking this, Lyu apologized.

"Why should I worry about you?"

But Ahnya made a stupid-looking expression—or rather a deeply confused one as she tilted her head.

"N-no…but you said I was depressed."

"Depressing things are depressing, meow. But Mama definitely uses elves roughly, too, so you'll forget about the things bothering you, meow."

Lyu went wide-eyed at her words.

"Look at Mei over there, meow. She also had a lot of things happen and looked suuuuper-depressed at first, but now she doesn't have the time for that, meow."

Ahnya pointed to one of the catgirl chefs. She was shorter than them, scampering around like a prum. She did not even have the time to adjust the chef's hat slipping off her head, a busy whirlwind as she moved around the kitchen.

"So feel free to feel down, as long as you get back up again, meow.

Everyone at this tavern was like that, meow. And you'll get there, too, meow."

She crudely and carelessly said this. She did not have any proof. However, her words made Lyu's heart feel several times lighter, so much so that she was jealous, wondering how much easier it would be if she could be like that.

"Ahnya…were you like that, too?" Lyu asked, suddenly curious.

"I—I…" The catgirl all of a sudden started to get flustered.

Her eyes darted to the left and right, making suspicious movements. The slender tail coming out of her back started quivering as though it could not stay still.

"I—I just remembered a chore, meow! I need to go for a bit, meow!" Awkwardly excusing herself, she disappeared.

Even that carefree girl had special circumstances. Lyu felt bad for bringing it up.

"Lyu, if you are back from the storehouse, then hurry up and come here."

She was briefly glancing in the direction that Ahnya had fled when Mia stuck her head into the kitchen and called her over.

"Next is washing the plates. Even a clumsy elf like you can do that, right?"

"…Understood."

Lyu nodded and headed over to the washing area. Noting the stacked-up tableware, she started washing them with water.

"…"

She dunked them over and over in a bucket of water. Soap bubbled, and the grime on the plates fell off. As the other girls carried over more dishes, she accepted them and kept moving her hands. Quietly, like a puppet.

Ahnya said all of that…But if the days continue like this, what should I do?

Lyu pondered her situation amid the squeaks of the plates she was wiping and the rush of flowing water in the washing area.

There is what Mia said. Eating delicious food is a good enough reason to live by itself. If that's true, then there's no reason for me to work here. Actually, I should probably get mad about this ridiculous maltreatment and leave. I could be free and do what I like.

In truth, now that she thought about trying to run away, she would be able to do so. But she didn't. It was not a sense of duty as a proud elf holding her back. It was because she did not have any goals to accomplish, and she had nowhere to go back to.

I already…don't have anything…

The emptiness of her revenge. The sense of loss from losing all her comrades. A hodgepodge of feelings dominated her heart. In an instant, her mind fell into darkness. The final support for her heart, the goddess Astrea, was no longer in Orario. Lyu herself had been the one who encouraged her to leave the city.

I cruelly forsook my own principles, and I've been stained and burned by the black flames. Why would she ever acknowledge me or let me live with her again?

She no longer had a home to return to.

And now I'm using this tavern in a vain attempt to avert my eyes…

I'm spending peaceful days working hard at a job I'm not used to, forgetting my emptiness temporarily. I'm depending on this idle life and calling it unavoidable as an excuse.

Acknowledging her feelings, Lyu recognized that much. She was not finding a goal. Not thinking about the future. Continuing to drag along her lost past. It was all just avoiding reality.

If I could find some other reason to stay at this place after—

"Lyu, can I help you?"

"…"

Lyu silently looked at Syr as she approached.

I see. It's because this girl is here.

Here was the reason that she could not break away from this tavern.

"…I'm okay. I'm not too busy, so you can do your own chores…"

"I've finished over here, so I thought I'd help out a bit? And this many dishes is pretty rough for one person."

Easily dodging Lyu's reservations, Syr lined up next to her. Lyu did not bother hiding her sigh. She had only known her for a little while, but she knew that it would be pointless to say more. They rinsed off the plates in the same wash area together.

Syr Flover…a person who took my hand.

Listening to another set of bubbles and water, Lyu glanced over at the girl. When she had collapsed in the back alley, Syr had grabbed Lyu's blood- and mud-covered hand. She had not rejected her, despite her elven tendency to prevent anyone she hadn't accepted to touch her skin, a deeply ingrained habit.

It's not as if I had acknowledged her…

There was no way she would be able to discern the character of someone she had only just met. That was obvious. She had just accepted the warmth of Syr's hand without reservations. As though she had felt the girl's kind spirit, or it was a fated meeting.

Just like Alizé.

That reality was what kept Lyu from trying to leave the tavern. She was the second special person to move her that way, and without realizing it, she could no longer do without her.

"Are you getting used to the job here?"

Lyu was stealing a glance at Syr when her heart jumped at the sudden question. Unusually flustered, she gave a long reply to cover it.

"A-a bit…but I'm still messing up a lot. I'm not as good at dealing with things as you are…"

"That's not true."

Syr smiled wryly as she shook her head. "I made all sorts of mistakes when I first started…Hmmm, probably even worse ones than you."

"…You did?"

"Yes. When the tavern employed me, back when I first started working."

Lyu was shocked. Syr stopped washing.

"At the beginning, I thought I could at least do this…but I broke a lot of plates, scorched lots of pots, messed up the ingredients I was supposed to buy…Mama Mia got really mad."

"…That's hard to believe."

Surprised, she was pulled into the girl's story. As far as she could tell, Syr was better than anyone else at all of the jobs in the tavern now.

"It would be nice to be able to say it was all a dream. But it's true. I'm still not very good at cooking."

She covered the bottom half of her face with the plate she was polishing as her cheeks slightly reddened, as if she was really embarrassed.

"When I got home, I'd dive into bed and whimper about how bad it was."

Hearing that, Lyu's lips opened a bit, and a soft chuckle escaped. Syr had shared an unexpected side of herself.

"—You finally laughed."

"?"

"Before that, you would never laugh. It seemed like you were always worried about something."

Lyu was surprised at the warmth in Syr's metallic-blue eyes. She looked back at the elf as she bashfully covered her mouth with one hand. Syr just innocently smiled.

I was able to laugh...

As Syr's cheerful smile faded, Lyu thought back.

It was like that before, too.

From Lyu's perspective, Syr had unnecessarily meddled countless times. Helping her with her work and even making it so she could work at the tavern in the first place. She had given the homeless Lyu shelter from the rain.

Ever since she had collapsed in that back alley, Syr's dedication had helped Lyu.

"...I..."

"?"

"I don't understand you."

As Syr tilted her head, Lyu turned to her.

"Why do you trouble yourself for me like that...? Why go so far? Are you trying to poke your nose into my business?"

She finally asked the questions that had been secretly lingering in her mind.

The girl who had drawn the smile out of her matched the elf's gaze. The clamor of the tavern continued: the footsteps of staff unhurriedly walking around, the bustle of food preparation from the kitchen, the conversations of customers eating with relish. Quietly watching Lyu, she finally smiled again.

"Lyu, come with me for a bit?"

Heading through The Benevolent Mistress's back entrance, they walked a bit into the back alleys. Proceeding through countless winding streets, up dozens of stairways, through arches and tunnels, they reached a building. An abandoned church. One of dozens of forgotten churches in the city's seventh district.

She brought Lyu to the roof of the building. When she crossed the threshold, she was wrapped in a brilliant light, and the sights of a peaceful town spread before her.

"Yep, it's another beautiful day!"

It was close to the blue sky. Syr raised a celebratory voice at the transparent blue canvas.

"Is it okay to leave the tavern without permission? If I do this, that dwarf owner might yell at me again…"

"You're always trying hard, so you can get away with a little."

Syr smiled like a mischievous little child. Lyu had recently come to realize that Syr was talented but a bit lacking in diligence from time to time. Almost like a breeze that could not be contained.

"…Then why did you bring me here?"

"Because it's my favorite spot. I wanted you to know about it, too."

The roof of the chapel was a bit higher than all the buildings around it, so it had a great view. Far off in the distance, Central Park was visible, and past that the still-sleeping Shopping District. Lyu could understand why it was her favorite place.

This reminds me of Alizé, also…

Her old friend had also liked high places. They had often gone to the roof of a building, surrounded by the lovely blue sky as they talked about the future.

However.

In Lyu's eyes now, that beautiful sky was also—.

—*Gray. It all looks gray.*

Not just the sky—everything looked colorless. That was what Lyu saw from her shroud of emptiness. As if everything she saw turned to gray.

Lyu's light green–dyed hair shook as she looked down.

"Higher than this is no good, and any lower wouldn't work, either. This is the only place where you can see all of Orario and still feel the presence of the people in the streets."

Perhaps recognizing Lyu's thoughts, or perhaps not, Syr continued talking as she looked out at the view.

"When you're here, you can understand what sorts of things the town is thinking."

"...Understand...the town's thoughts?"

"Yep. The people holding their head high as they walk, the carriage dashing through Main Street...the adventurers' arguments, and the children's laughter."

Lyu looked up at Syr's back as she continued speaking.

"For years, Orario was always sad, scared..."

"..."

Orario's Dark Age. The rise of evil that had been the source of the Evils had brought fear and mayhem to the city. Blood flowed in the endless cycle of destruction. Many non-adventurers were lost, too. Having stood on the front lines where chaos and order clashed, Lyu felt her heart hurt when she thought of the residents of the city still living in fear. She was filled with shame and a desire to apologize.

"But, you know, lately it's different."

"Eh?"

"The town is gradually starting to be able to smile. They can celebrate and be happy."

As Lyu's eyes went wide, Syr turned around, and said:

"That's thanks to you guys, isn't it?"

"—"

Lyu was at a loss for words as Syr smiled.

"*Ganesha Familia*, *Loki Familia*, *Freya Familia*...and also *Astrea*

Familia. You and lots of other adventurers fought, were hurt, and still kept trying…and you protected the people."

Several familias had been established in order to subdue the Evils. They all had their own intentions, but they had fought the followers of the evil gods in order to drive away the darkness covering Orario. Lyu's *Astrea Familia* had also stood for justice and continued to fight to protect people's smiles. They had tried to destroy evil. And Lyu's own blade had brought an end to it.

"The neighborhood is peaceful thanks to what you all did. That's why I have to try to find some happiness for you, too."

"—"

"If the person who worked the hardest isn't happy………Well, I don't like that."

"You're wrong! Wrong!" Lyu shouted back. "When my friends were killed, I wasn't fighting for peace! That wasn't justice anymore! I just lost my temper for a personal grudge, to get revenge…!"

And the result was this. In the end I got my name on the blacklist, and I've incurred the wrath and resentment of lots of people.

Syr continued to smile at Lyu, who had acted as judge, jury, and executioner for the criminals throughout Orario who were suspected of a connection with the Evils.

"Even so, the adventurers who come to the tavern say it…even the gods say it. 'Orario was reborn.'"

As if saying "Look," she pointed to a street corner below where a performance was happening. On one corner of the main street, a band was playing a song honoring a valorous adventurer. It would have been impossible to imagine such a scene when evil was rampant and public order was crumbling.

Lyu was speechless.

She had missed it while consumed by the flames of revenge. Something she had not noticed as she grieved for her friend and the comrades who had lost their lives, moaning that there was nothing left.

Something still remained of Alizé and the rest: the fruits of their labor. What Lyu had managed to accomplish was compensation for her friends' lives.

"I'll say it for everyone else, okay?"

As Lyu struggled for words, Syr gazed into her eyes and smiled.

"You fought so hard for us...Thank you."

When she heard those words, a single tear silently spilled from Lyu's eye.

"Now, everyone is able to smile."

Syr looked out across the neighborhood one more time.

The wind carried the voices of laughing children, just like an ordinary peaceful town. If she listened closely, she felt sure that she could sense the feelings of the town.

The feelings of the people who lived here.

I...

In the midst of everyone's feelings, Lyu thought she heard a certain voice. An imagined voice amid the others.

She could sense the smiles of Alizé and her friends living on in the town.

Their soft whispers—*In our stead...*

I...I have to make sure of it myself, I think.

She would have to watch over their legacy in their stead. That was what Lyu thought.

She had decided on a future she wanted to set out for.

The sky...

As the world turned watery through her tears, the surrounding skies cleared up. Like a forest sprouting new leaves all at once, the gray disappeared, and the beautiful blue color returned.

Lyu realized that the heart she had thought was empty now held something. Her tears fell again.

...She's a mysterious person.

Wiping her eyes, she looked at Syr, who was gazing out over the town. She had unraveled Lyu's feelings just like Astrea—like a goddess of compassion.

I acknowledge her. Her meddling—her words—brought me back on to my path.

Just what is she?

As Lyu stared at her, Syr turned around and broke into a smile.

"Your eyes became really pretty."

"...If you think so, then it's only thanks to you."

"Really? I'm glad. I like people like you...People who can become beautiful for someone else's sake."

As if Lyu was too radiant to look at, Syr's metallic-blue eyes squinted into a smile, her cheeks blushing in delight for an instant.

"What will you do now? If you've found what you want to do, then you don't need to force yourself to stay at the tavern, you know? I can talk to Mama Mia for you."

"I..."

She paused for a second before straightforwardly acknowledging her answer.

"I want to repay you."

I want to repay you for letting me notice what Alizé left behind. For letting me see this beautiful blue sky again.

Those were Lyu's true feelings.

"...Is that okay?"

"Yes. If not for you, my friends would have let me have it."

Without a doubt.

Thinking that, Lyu's face relaxed. As the girl gazed in surprise, a small, neat, flower-like smile appeared on Lyu's face. Syr grinned broadly.

"Well then, I'm glad you'll keep working with me at the tavern."

"Understood. It's not like I have anywhere else to go. I'll burden you for a bit longer."

"Yep. I look forward to it, Lyu."

Surrounded by the sky, they smiled like old friends, the blue sky warmly watching over them.

"About time to head back?"

"Yes."

At Syr's prompt, Lyu nodded. Lyu looked back one last time in order to etch the scene of the beautiful sky and town into her memory as she left the roof, exiting the deserted church with Syr.

She headed back, wrapped in a warm feeling that she did not have when she had arrived. Before long, she could see The Benevolent Mistress.

Her eyes leaped to the people loitering in front of the tavern's rear entrance. It was Ahnya and the rest of the employees.

"Ahnya? Why are you here?"

"Fufun. I saw that you guys were ditching work, so we wanted to congratulate you, meow!"

"Aren't you just procrastinating?"

Ahnya responded to Syr's question with an odd pride, but she yelped and turned red at Lyu's observation. However, she stared at Lyu's face and then smiled cheerfully.

"I like that expression better, meow."

"...Yes. I stopped being so gloomy."

Lyu smiled slightly back. The other catgirls besides Ahnya looked on happily. The procrastination was just an excuse. Lyu understood that they were waiting for her to come back after Syr had taken her out.

"No more going easy on you, meow! You're a rival, not just a stray we took in, meow! You better be prepared to put your jaw into it, meow!"

"Back, Ahnya?"

Ignoring Syr's gentle correction, Ahnya moved closer to Lyu.

"Which is to say, let's try shaking hands again, meow!"

This is what she's been after.

The catgirl triumphantly put out her right hand, and Lyu's hand made as if to grab it. Just as she was about to do that—*slap!* She knocked the hand away with all of her strength. The atmosphere froze.

...Crap...

Lyu's hand had reflexively moved as she started to sweat. Even someone as insensitive to people's feelings as Lyu could understand. The carefully constructed pleasantness had been wrecked. While time stopped for Syr and the other staff, she timidly peeked at Ahnya...and saw a savage cat with a blazing fire behind her eyes.

"I'll definitely touch you, meow...!"

"W—"

Lyu was agitated as the stubborn catgirl started talking big.

These catgirls are annoying in an entirely different way from Alizé and the rest—!

Lyu was sure of that as Ahnya gradually slipped into a stance, staring daggers at her.

"Haah!"

"Wha—Syr?!"

Syr had suddenly hugged her.

"You let me touch you."

"L-let me go!"

Syr did not seem to mind as Lyu turned red. Wrapping both arms around her neck, she put her cheek on Lyu's.

"Myaaaaaaa! Why am I bad and Syr's okay, meow? That's impossible! This is a matter of pride, meow!!"

"—!"

"Fugya!"

Lyu countered, Ahnya was sent flying, and Syr laughed aloud. The rest of the staff all started clapping and laughing along, too.

"...Hey, you stupid girls! Ain't every last one of you skipping work?!"

Watching from afar, Mia's eyes narrowed, and finally she bellowed at them as their horseplay continued.

Lyu thought.

Syr and the other staff were not a replacement for Alizé and the rest. Believing something like that would be a disservice to these girls. And the grief and emptiness from losing irreplaceable comrades was not so easily healed. Even if it healed, unexpected twinges could bring back Lyu's loneliness.

However, I have to move forward. Even if I remember the past, I can only move forward. Together with Alizé's legacy.

* * *

She decided to write a letter. One addressed to the goddess she had been separated from.

What I'm doing and what I've decided...If this ever gets delivered, she'll know. She would definitely smile when she reads it.

Returning to The Benevolent Mistress alongside Ahnya and the rest, she secretly whispered to the girl who had helped her, who had constantly meddled and led her to discover so many things.

"Thank you, Syr...I'm grateful."

3

The evening sun set beyond the western wall.

Surrounded by the gigantic city wall, Orario's darkness came early. Runoa had learned that much, having come to this Labyrinth City almost four years ago.

"...She's changed."

West Main Street was tinted red. In the middle of a street crowded with adventurers returning from the Dungeon and laborers whose jobs were over for the day, she had stopped and looked over at The Benevolent Mistress. The elf staff girl was reflected in her eyes.

Gale Wind...Her expression is softer now.

She was still awkward at her job. She was still not very good at customer service. But after observing the situation several days ago, Runoa could tell that Gale Wind's face had changed a bit. Before, she always looked as though she was forcing herself and darkness clouded her face.

Her aura had suggested she'd lost someone important, or maybe lost her path.

But it was different now. She was holding her head high, her dignified figure exuding vitality like a large tree in a forest. A spark of determination had returned to her sky-blue eyes, and she sometimes smiled ever so slightly when her colleagues called out to her.

Ahhh...she found a place she belongs.

As if feeling her gaze, Gale Wind turned toward her.

Exchanging glances through the window, Runoa puller her scarf up over her mouth and started moving with the crowd again, heading away from the tavern.

Betrayed is maybe a bit much, but...maybe, recently, I felt like we were alike.

Walking along Main Street, Runoa noticed that she was jealous of Gale Wind.

"Family, friends, familia...I don't have any of that."

Looking up at the twilight sky, she spoke to herself.

Being alone in a crowd of people like this brought back old memories.

—Runoa Faust was born in a certain territory of the empire, far from Orario. Before she was old enough to understand what was happening, she lost her parents in the war that led to the country serving the empire, so she became a street urchin, fending for herself without anyone's protection. Between theft, fights, and turf wars with other street kids, a day did not go by without some new bruises.

For Runoa at the time, it was obvious to jump at the opportunity to join a familia as soon as she found out about them and the Falna she could be granted. It was just that important to have power. If she could join one, she would not have to worry about the bare necessities like food or shelter. After she had a Status, her physical strength increased to a new level. Runoa's struggle to survive became significantly easier.

The head god of the familia was a confusing guy. Later she heard that he amused himself with a coup d'état and revolution game. She had never really understood his will and did not enjoy how he used his followers like pawns. Maybe he had loved them, but she did not really understand it.

In the end, it collapsed into infighting, and the familia was destroyed.

—After that, she began drifting from place to place like tumbleweed.

There wasn't a twilight like this in the imperial territory where I grew up.

For Runoa, such an unfettered life was alluring and exciting. She started collecting bounties in order to earn money for traveling. Whenever she remembered to, she would provisionally join an appropriate familia and have her Status updated. She had already had three conversions. She had never really joined a particular familia.

Outside the city—outside Orario—a difference in Level was absolute. Unlike the Labyrinth City, which boasted the Dungeon, people who could level up were few and far between. The only places that could lay claim to multiple people of Level 3 and higher were famous cities and countries like the Empire or the Great Country of Magic, the handful of world powers. With her talent for fighting, Runoa leveled up quickly and was acknowledged as superior wherever she went—but became isolated.

Her time in her first familia had made her stronger by leaps and bounds. Rough as she was, she provoked animosity and jealousy in her colleagues, so she was not familiar with the concept of comrades. She thought she was fine with that. She took pride in her ability to get by on her own strength. That was why she had decided making friends was unnecessary.

—But I was out of my element here.

Three years ago, she had the opportunity to come to Orario. The Labyrinth City was different from anywhere else in the world she had seen. She did not know how it would look in a few years or a few decades. But Orario at the turning point of the Dark Age was a scary place. Back then, the clash of justice and evil, as well as the powers attempting to use that clash, led to countless formidable forces squaring off around the city known as the Center of the World. So many strong people were fighting like madmen to fulfill their desires and wishes.

Coming to that place by herself, Runoa was swallowed up by the raging waves of the period.

—The first time I thought I might die was probably when I got the contract for Freya Familia.

Once, she had targeted an adventurer belonging to a certain beautiful goddess's faction, but the tables were turned on her. She ran for her life from four terrifying prums, just barely escaping alive.

For the girl who had boasted of her invincibility outside the city, her first total defeat was only the first shock.

I knew that Orario was dangerous, but I still jumped in. I can't deny that it was mostly just a carefree desire to test my strength. I never thought they would be so monstrous.

Biting back her humiliation, she started to pick and chose her jobs. She fought and fought, and the struggles never ended. By nature, she hated to lose, and whenever she was wounded, she would scream and flail in frustration. She leveled up a third time. But it was endless. Adventurers stronger than her kept appearing one after the other. She would do in a target and get a large reward, but she still did not feel better.

Before I knew, being alone became tiring.

For the den of demons that was Orario, *solitude* was a poison that ate away at your body.

It was imperative not to go it alone. She had struggled to get this far, but she was reaching her limit.

Just like the Dungeon that could only be challenged with a party, Orario was merciless to solo wanderers.

"...It's exhausting, really..."

Looking back on the days leading up to now, Runoa sighed, wallowing in a sentimentality that was unlike her.

Some of it was the light shock at seeing that Gale Wind had found a place she belonged, but the source of it was the *exhaustion*. She was tired. Tired of being alone.

Thinking along those lines as she walked among the crowds coming and going on Main Street, all of a sudden—

"Oh...Runoa?"'

A goddess appeared. She had buoyant, long, honey-colored hair. She was holding a paper bag to her impossibly large breasts, clearly returning from shopping. Her kindly, rounded eyes sparkled with surprise. One of her followers was beside her as protection. Surprised at running into her in this crowd, Runoa whispered her name.

"Demeter..."

"That surprised me, I didn't think I'd meet you in a place like that."

"Me, too."

A room in *Demeter Familia*'s home, Wheat Hall, in the north of Orario. There, at Demeter's invitation, Runoa had taken her top off and was naked from the waist up.

"I had wanted to ask you to check my Status, so it was perfect timing."

"You only come to see me when you need your blessing renewed. You can come anytime, you know?"

Runoa forced a laugh as Demeter examined at her back with a pout.

Demeter pricked her fingertip with a needle, dripping ichor on Runoa's back while she sat on a chair. In the blink of an eye, a hieroglyph list appeared, and a new inscription was added.

Runoa had contracted with Demeter. In other words, *Demeter Familia* was her fifth membership.

"The hall is quiet. How are Persephone and the rest?"

"It's harvest time, so almost all of the children are in the fields outside the city. The sun's set, so they'll be coming back soon, I think."

It was random chance that Runoa had contracted with Demeter. When she came to Orario hunting bounties, her Status eventually became out of date. While she was looking for a suitable group, she had bumped into Demeter as she had today and asked for help. From Runoa's perspective, the carefree, gentle-seeming Demeter seemed like a goddess of good character and had been easy to negotiate with.

In particular, *Demeter Familia* was a commerce-oriented faction, running the farms producing wheat, vegetables, fruits, and the like. She figured that she would not end up in a fight if she was in a non-martial faction, even if she messed up.

"All right, you're updated."

"Thank you, Demeter."

Taking the update report that had been translated into Koine, Runoa started reading it without bothering to cover her chest.

Runoa Faust

LEVEL 4

Strength: B 704 -> 780 Defense: C 660 -> B 722
Dexterity: D 545 -> 577 Agility: D 559 -> 599 Magic: I 0
Punch: H Crush: I Brawler: I

I've been neglecting it for a while, but still…it rose a pretty good amount…

She should have been pleased with what was a good amount of growth for a Level 4, but Runoa was tired. She fully understood how monstrous Orario could be, so all she could manage was a sigh to herself. Borrowing a candle, she immediately burned the paper with her secret Status on it and fixed her clothes.

"Runoa. You're going to have dinner, right?"

"Ah, no, I…"

"I planned a feast today. I'm sure I made too much, so there will be food left over. Will you help me? Persephone also wanted to meet you."

Intending to turn down Demeter's kindness, Runoa was overcome by the goddess's gentle smile. She scratched her cheek as Demeter started the preparations for tea.

Strictly speaking, Runoa was a follower of Demeter, but not a member of her familia. It was just for the purposes of updating her Status—Runoa was free to convert at any time. Runoa had intended to listen to any requests Demeter had in return, but the goddess who ruled over fertility had only smiled cheerfully without asking for anything.

© NIRITSU

Speaking bluntly, it was a convenient place for Runoa to update her Status.

That had made her feel a little guilty, and she still felt rather bad about it.

"Before we eat—here, pie and cookies. It's just the leftovers from yesterday, though."

Dessert before dinner, huh? It must be nice to be a goddess who can't get fat. Runoa looked suspiciously at Demeter's always-thin waist and enormous, jiggling chest as she reached out to take the handmade treats: a tomato pie, which replaced apples with vegetables, and wheat cookies. The tomatoes in the pie were as sweet as strawberries, and the wheat in the cookies was mixed with herbs to draw out the sweetness.

"Mmm…delicious. Your food is amazing like always. Have you considered opening a restaurant?"

"No way! If you praise me too much, it'll go to my head."

Laughing, Demeter made black tea. Runoa smiled unconsciously at her warmth. She enjoyed this time. The only place in Orario that Runoa could feel like this was here.

"Is your 'job' still busy?"

"…Yeah, I have one big job left. But I was thinking this should be my last one. I'm getting a little tired…"

Demeter had never asked what Runoa did. There was no way she should have figured it out. But she would sometimes let her have these calm moments, with those kind eyes as though she were consoling a child.

If it were not for Demeter, Runoa might have collapsed long ago.

"After you stop, what will you do?"

"…"

"Hey, Runoa? If you're interested…why not raise wheat, vegetables, and fruit with us? It's rather hard work, but it's really worthwhile, you know?"

Runoa stared in a daze as Demeter smiled across the table. She had actually considered maybe joining *Demeter Familia*. Among all the gods she had dealt with up to now, Demeter was the best to work with, and the group members who followed her were friendly. And she felt like a place to return to like this would feel pretty nice.

But Runoa did not do it...

"Thanks, Demeter...but I can't."

"Runoa..."

"I just don't think I can do something like that."

Runoa held her hand up and stared at the back of it.

"You've seen my Status, so you've probably figured it out I think, but...I do rough work. I beat people up, spill lots of blood..."

"..."

"My hands...are really dirty."

Runoa's alias was Black Fist. The origin of the name was not the gauntlets she used. It was another name used by people in the underworld in fear at the blackish red stains on her fists from tearing flesh, breaking bone, and spilling blood by the gallon. Runoa could see her knuckles tainted with blood, her hands colored black by beating so many people.

"Wheat, vegetables, and fruit...you work hard to nurture them so that people get to eat them, right? They bring joy to so many, too...If my hands got involved...Yeah, they would probably taste bad."

That was the reason she had kept my distance from *Demeter Familia*. If other people found out that Black Fist was connected to Demeter and the familia, her reputation might tarnish theirs.

After meeting Demeter, she had not accepted any contracts aimed at the faction the goddess supported, the familias affiliated with the Guild. Though no one else knew that.

Bounty hunters were similar to the mercenaries contributing to the city's turmoil, so it was natural they would be the targets of animosity.

"I'm sorry, Demeter. I should go. Thank you for the pie and cookies."

"Runoa, we..."

"It's okay. Really. I'm going to wash my hands of it after this job."

Standing up from her chair, she put on a full-spirited smile for the sad-looking Demeter. It hurt Runoa to make her worry. It would probably be best to abandon this last job.

But she would not.

Probably, this would be a ceremony that would allow her to break with her bounty hunter past, her new beginning, and also a means to vent her anger.

She felt a childish resentment toward Gale Wind, who had bathed just as much blood as her but still found a place to belong while Runoa had not.

A self-deprecating smirk crossed her face for an instant before she put on a brave smile for Demeter and left the room.

"And if I'm just gonna be hanging out, I should probably do it with idiots like me instead of you guys."

The light from the sea of magic-stone lamps shone brighter than the stars above.

It was hard to see the stars at night in sleepless Orario. Chloe had come to understand that since she had come to the Labyrinth City almost four years ago.

"...She's changed, meow."

Evening settled on West Main Street.

She was staring down at The Benevolent Mistress from a moonlit roof. She was looking down on the elf employee who had just thrown out an adventurer.

Gale Wind...You're a different person from just a little while ago, meow.

She had spectacularly tossed an adventurer who had made a pass at one of her coworkers out of the building, and she had received a round of applause. She looked hard to deal with, but the smile she directed at the platinum-haired girl she just helped was like a flower emerging from melted snow.

No...she's returned to how she was, meow.

As if sensing Chloe's presence, her sky-blue eyes looked up.

Wearing a hood low over her eyes, Chloe suddenly flipped over like a stray cat. She soundlessly crossed the roof and landed in the shadowy backstreet.

"You found a place you belong, meow?"

She spoke to herself in the empty, dark alley, her cat ears making two little peaks in her hood.

She took Gale Wind's information sheet out of her breast pocket. The Guild had not released this likeness of the mask-wearing adventurer, and they didn't know her face. This bounty that had been put out by adventurers and merchants.

Gale Wind had gone too far. She had incurred the wrath of too many people and now had a bounty on her head.

If you can make a face like that then…if you've found a place you belong in the daylight, at least be a bit smarter about it, she thought.

She sighed with a heavy heart as she trudged along.

"If you're going to mature, there are easier ways, meow…"

People could be tenacious about clinging to life. Sometimes that made the job hard to do. She knew that from firsthand experience dating back to just after she was born.

—Chloe Lolo had been a member of a criminal familia that was whispered of in secret all around the continent.

Before she was even given the name *Chloe*, she had to perform a job in order to join the familia. How to handle poison, how to build resistance to it, how to use a knife—she was taught all of it from birth. With a starting point like that, developing a logical point of view was hopeless from the start. If she took out a target whose name she did not know by pretending to be an innocent little girl, she was praised. If she took poison and just barely survived, writhing in agony, she was praised… Life was probably most pleasant when she did not know anything.

The familia I belonged too, well, they were pretty much garbage.

The deity who established it called it role-playing.

"If there are guys who want dirty jobs done, then there's no way around it. I'll wear the mud." Cheerfully saying such absurdities, the patron deity sowed blood and death through the underworld—garbage presiding over slaughter.

She eventually got fed up with the familia when an assassin who was like an older sister to her—the mother who had given birth to her and watched over her without ever sharing her secret—messed up on a mission and died. Going against the rules of the organization, she had lost her life shielding Chloe.

Learning the truth later, Chloe also discovered how useless tears were. Doubting the organization and rebelling against the rules, she told the founding goddess she wanted to quit. Chloe could still remember her smirk even now.

Her ceremonial assignment to be able to leave was an unreasonable string of deadly demands to test her resolve. She had almost fainted when she was told to take out a certain empire's Level 3 upper-tier knight with a single knife. But Chloe had done it. Thanks to that, she leveled up, too. The goddess was trash, but she was honest enough to uphold a contract signed in blood.

—*Well, what I'm doing didn't really change much, though.*

Chloe had gained her freedom, but she was still lost.

She did not know what she should do. She did not know what she should live for. Knowing nothing but how to kill people, she was missing something. She was damaged.

If you traced back the secret to her success to its source, it lay in the expressions and tone of voice she had learned just mimicking ridiculous gods.

If I hadn't adopted this stupid speech pattern and personality, I wouldn't have been able to do it. The real Chloe that no one ever saw was scared, a crybaby.

In the end, the business she had chosen was assassination.

One kill, lots of money. For earning cash quickly and efficiently, there was no other choice.

There was a relatively large number of vermin in the world. So it was rare that a job would bother her. Sometimes, she was even like a chivalrous thief and became a hero for orphans to mimic. That was a pretty pleasant. Particularly the soft feeling of getting hugged by little boys. That was around when her sexual inclinations started to twist, and she started becoming filled with desire.

—*I was sure there was no one who could stop me.*

Thinking back on it, Chloe had gotten carried away when she waltzed into Orario.

It had the worst public order in the world at the time, and stepping into that city unconcerned about jobs and without taking it seriously was the first mistake. Orario was a den of thieves. The stronghold of adventurers, sealed in those giant city walls. Chloe had just been a *big fish in a little pond*. The cat who did not know the depths of the abyss known as the Dungeon received a baptism from the monsters born and tempered there.

—The first time I thought, "Ah, I'm dead!" was when I took a contract on Ganesha Familia, *meow.*

When she tried to target a certain adventurer in the elephant god's faction, she almost got herself killed. She ran for her life from the terrifying heroine known as Ankusha.

For the girl who had boasted of a perfect kill record outside the Labyrinth City, it was the first frustration, the first failure.

The difference in strength between Orario and the outside world was exceedingly large; it was not something Chloe could measure with tools she had gained from the familia that had raised her.

Remembering the fear that made her tail stand on end, Chloe started picking her jobs carefully.

Her assassinations had rules.

First, she would not kill children. Especially little boys who were the treasure of the world. Robbing the world of that treasure was unthinkable.

Also, she would only kill people who were human filth, or else were mentally prepared to die. If a target broke either of those rules, she would throw the client's money back and cancel the job.

Fortunately, if it could really be called that, she had never had to cancel a job once (though she had failed before). As if to mock the supposed upheaval of the Dark Age, the contracts that made their way to Chloe were generally just thugs taking each other out or groups throwing their weight around in their power struggles. Laughing bitterly at the pointlessness of it, Chloe easily completed those jobs. She leveled up again and was now Level 4.

However, no matter how many she killed, assassination contracts never ended.

The rewards were gold coins: chips in exchange for red drops of life.

Just how much blood have I soaked this blade in?

She had gotten here on inertia alone. Or possibly, what little pride Chloe had had not allowed her to stop.

However, her heart was starting to get melancholy. She was used to being alone due to the nature of her work, but more and more, she found herself wanting a place to rest. A place she belonged, like Gale Wind.

Under the starry sky, she held up her assassin's knife to the moon, soaking in her emotions in a way that was unlike her.

"I'm tired, meow..."

Sighing, Chloe put away her knife as she sensed the presence of another person. Leaving the backstreet, she turned onto Southwest Main Street. Lost in thought for a long time, she had wandered so far south that she had ended up here.

Resting her shoulders on a wall, she casually watched the flow of people.

"Meow?"

She noticed a certain god.

His brown hair was pulled back behind his head. His masculine face was a prime example of a good-looking man. He wasn't wearing a top even though it was halfway into fall already, which brought the phrase "man of the sea" to mind. Next to him, a follower was helping by pulling a luggage cart.

"...Mya-ha!"

Recognizing his figure in the midst of the crowd, an evil smile crossed Chloe's face.

She leaped out the next instant, jumping onto him.

"Guoh?! Wh-what?!...Guh, Chloe Lolo."

While his helper was shocked, the god murmured the name of the person who was clinging to his back. His face twitched. Chloe smiled suspiciously as she also responded to the person she had happened to notice in the crowded road.

"Long time, no see, Njörðr. You doing well?"

* * *

"Maaan, I'm lucky, meow. Since we bumped into each other, you're treating me to a drink, meow."

"You're just dragging me along..."

A room in a high-class bar in the Shopping District that covered southern Orario.

In a sound-proofed individual room, alone with Njörðr, Chloe had stripped down to just one piece of underwear.

"By the way, why do you always undress completely when you show me your Status...?"

"That's rude, meow. I'm wearing panties, meow! It's just so I can keep up with your exhibitionism, meow!"

Like a certain bounty hunter, Chloe had converted and contracted with Njörðr. He was the god who ruled over the fish who lived in Port Meren to the southwest of Orario.

The faction he managed was in the fishing business, operating in the ocean, starting at the brackish Lolog Lake that connected with Meren. They repeatedly went out to sea to catch lots of fish. The fresh seafood caught by *Njörðr Familia* was sold in Orario, and just like the agriculture managed by *Demeter Familia*, it made a big impact on the city's food situation.

He had apparently come from Meren today with his followers to sell seafood. The fisherman who had been helping him out until earlier had already headed back.

The reason why Chloe had contracted with Njörðr, who lived outside the city...

"Is it okay to take a tone like that, meow? Should I expose your smuggling, meow?"

"Guh...!"

It was because of that.

Thanks to one of her jobs, Chloe had infiltrated a suspicious place and happened to see Njörðr taking freight from a shady group to secretly smuggle into the city.

He had apparently helped out with the smuggling on the condition

© NIRITSU

that it was *necessary for the fish*, but Chloe did not know the details. Even without knowing, it was still sufficient for extortion.

Thanks to that, Chloe got a convenient, handsome way to update her Status, and Njörðr was not in a position to resist with her holding that over him.

"I can't update my Status if I'm not like this, meow~."

Lying down on the soft sofa, she gave the impression of a queen. She was enjoying herself since he had covered the high fee to get into the tavern. The god grimaced as he moved beside her to update her Status.

A secret room with a half-naked god and mostly naked girl.

If a waitress brought the alcohol now, she would unquestionably misunderstand what was going on.

"Because you are such a good, handsome god, I'm letting you see this unladylike figure, meow. My lovely nude body honed for assassination...Does it take your breath away, meow?"

"Take my breath away...? Your chest is flatter than mine."

"What?! I'm just still developing, meow!"

As an assassin, there were times I also used my feminine wiles. Well, only idiot targets were done in like that, though. Truly wary men were usually on guard.

—Incidentally, when Chloe had been about to do it for real once, she scratched her partner's face, so she was still a virgin.

"There, it's done."

"Grrr...you'll pay for that, meow."

Miffed, Chloe took the update sheet and looked at it.

Chloe Lolo

LEVEL 4

Strength: G 267 -> F 301 Defense: G 222 -> 279

Dexterity: B 711 -> 751 Agility: B 737 -> 776 Magic: E 412 -> 455

Immunity: G Synthesis: H Escape: I

It's been a while, but still…it's gone up a good amount, meow.

She sighed.

Doing people in without too much effort was supposed to be what assassins did, but her Status continuing to rise was proof of a lot of hard work.

"So? If you got an update, does that mean Black Cat got another troublesome request?"

"Please don't call me that name, meow. As far as I'm concerned, it's a blemish on my record, meow."

Code name aside, having a second name or alias from other people was proof of failure to an assassin. Having a second name made meant that an assassination failed or that someone had seen her. This was all because the adventurers in Orario were too strong…

Being compared to a bounty hunter like Black Fist is a real nuisance, Chloe thought.

"Hey…you're tired, right?"

"…"

As expected of a god, he had figured her out and seen what she was feeling in her heart. Chloe silently got off the sofa and grabbed the food on the table with her fingers in a show of poor manners.

"In times like this, that's how it has to be, meow."

"If you feel like it, why don't you come to my familia?"

Chloe froze for a second and then tried to cover it with a suggestive smile.

"What's that? Have you been captivated by my beauty and fallen prey to your desires, meow?"

"Aah, yeah, something like that would fine. If I got my hands on a cute female helper like you, the gods would rejoice."

Njörðr responded to her teasing with a wry laugh, meeting her eyes with a concerned gaze.

Njörðr is a good god.

He's handsome, tall, and cares for children. He's a god of good character.

While knowing the true identity of Black Cat, he had not revealed it to anyone, and while he complained about it, he still put up with her selfish and absurd requests, as if he was trying to give her a brief moment to relax.

After being quiet for a bit, she smiled slightly in a way that was different from before.

"You should stop that, meow. A cat who stopped killing people and reformed to be crazy about fish…it's kind of ridiculous, meow."

"…I see."

That was how she truly felt.

She was honestly happy at his offer, but she could not quite see herself taking it.

"And familia aside…I don't really understand things like comrades and friends, meow."

That was also how she really felt.

With no interactions since her first familia, she was a lonely stray cat. She did not know how to go about joining a group.

That's way harder than killing people, she thought.

"Is there anyone who gets along well from the start? No, it starts with conflict. You shout at each other; you want to punch each other."

"You gods are always talking about 'fighting under the sunset'; is that what this is, meow? But as for me, I don't even know how to do that much, meow…"

Chloe's bread and butter was deadly fights. Alive or dead were the only options she knew.

She could not face Njörðr, who was kindly gazing at her as he tried to convince her. She suddenly looked up at the ceiling. She said the thought that popped into her head.

"But, you know…if there was someone who could fight me with all their strength, come at me to kill…and still crack jokes with me…it would be nice to be that carefree, meow."

They held many feelings in their hearts.

However, they would soon encounter each other.

* * *

"When are you going to do in Gale Wind? Think about how many days have passed since you took the contract."

"You're annoying. I got it already."

The client had called Runoa out to pester her. Glaring back at him in the tavern on the outskirts of the outskirts, she laid out her plan.

"Let me be clear: I'm washing my hands of everything after this job. I want a promise from you guys at the Bruno Corporation to not get involved with me again after this."

"...Thinking you can return to an honest life after all this?"

"I don't know anything. But if I don't make a start, nothing will happen."

She responded clearly as the human from the corporation scowled.

"Don't worry, I'll do the job. Just wait and I'll finish her, like I always do."

Adjusting her scarf, she announced with a piercing gaze:

"Tomorrow night—that's when it starts."

"Black Fist is targeting Gale Wind, it seems! She even said she would do it tomorrow! What should we do?"

"Mmm~, this is bad timing."

In a forgotten belfry, a concerned client's voice echoed. Chloe had been called out here; she used her business tone and slowly replied.

"Competing for prey...These times are really exhausting."

"What are you saying so casually? If we don't get her quickly, they'll get there first!"

The dwarf's voice came at her from both sides as the hood she wore low over her eyes shook. Chloe understood why she was so tired. It was because Orario was stagnating in darkness. After experiencing so much darkness, she knew that it had borne more swirling malice, more chaos than any other country or city she had seen before.

"...But even that is done."

By none other than Gale Wind's hand. Orario had been reborn. Chloe felt that.

"Who'd have thought I'd get stuck taking out Gale Wind…? What an unpleasant job."

"O-oh?"

"Relax. A job's a job, and I already took the prepayment, so I won't ditch the contract."

While the client lost his composure as though he were seriously getting scared, she reminded him that she was a professional.

The existence of Gale Wind was a breeding ground for future troubles.

People who resented her would probably come at her with malicious intent some point. So her disappearing now was for the sake of the future.

Arming herself with that pretext, Chloe steeled her resolve.

"Tomorrow night, I'll do her in."

4

"…"

Moving through the hallway of the side building, Lyu stopped and looked out the window.

The early morning sky was cloudy.

Gray was covering the whole sky, creating a disquieting feeling.

I'm being watched…

Since she had started working at The Benevolent Mistress, Lyu had felt someone *watching* her. At first the gaze did not include hostility or malice—more exhaustion—so Lyu had written it off as a non-problem, but at this point she could clearly sense the intent behind it.

Namely, bloodlust.

I didn't think it was a pursuer…but clearly my intuition was off.

A gaze like that had only one explanation. Someone had tracked down Gale Wind. The misgivings she had about getting Syr and the rest wrapped up in this by letting them shelter her had come to fruition. And just when she had been taken on as an official employee of the tavern.

At this rate, I'm going to cause trouble for The Benevolent Mistress... for Syr and the others.

Those thoughts in her mind, Lyu silently started moving into the side building. She headed toward Mia's room.

"Pardon me. I'm sorry, I need to talk......Syr?"

She had knocked and started to open the door when she saw Syr in the room with Mia. Unlike Lyu and the other girls, Syr did not live in the side building. Lyu was surprised to Mia's unexpected visitor so early in the day.

"Good morning, Lyu."

"...Good morning, Syr."

"What do you want this early?"

Nodding, Lyu walked over to the two. As Lyu was about to start, Mia cut in.

"You're about to say something like 'I'm sorry since you just employed me, but I'd like you to let me quit,' aren't ya?"

"!"

"Sheesh...Don't get jumpy just because some people started coming sniffing around for *you*."

Lyu was caught off guard as Mia just shook her head and crossed her arms.

"...It's too soon to say if they have figured me out. But me being here will cause problems for—"

"I've had nothing but problems since we first brought you here, idiot."

"Guh!"

Mia brazenly looked down on Lyu, not letting her string two thoughts together.

"The one who hired you is me. And this bar and all the employees here are mine. I won't allow any of them to up and disappear on me."

Lyu was bewildered as Mia gave a shocking reply.

"Lyu, we finally got to work together, so separating would be lonely."

"Syr...but..."

"It's okay. Mama aside, Ahnya and the others are strong, too. This place is safer than any other place you could go." Syr entreated her to stay and then smiled.

Lyu had already gathered that this restaurant was far stronger than the average familia. Not just Mia individually, either; all of the staff that had special circumstances were highly skilled. What Syr said was likely true.

Even so, Lyu kept hesitating, with "buts" and "howevers" and endless excuses.

"Don't be so hesitant. I always knew this time would come. If you don't want to cause problems for us, then just work hard and pay what you owe."

The giant dwarf poked the elf's chest with a thump. Lyu winced at hearing such an absurd thing...but after a pause, she smiled.

"Understood...I started this. I'll handle it somehow or another."

She was happy that Mia and Syr treated her almost as if she was a member of a familia. Just as she felt that, her stomach rumbled. Syr and Mia both started laughing.

"Speaking of, what did you come to talk about this early in the morning?"

"About that...Tonight, we have errands, me and Syr. The bar won't run without the two of us, so we are closing for the night."

"Errands? Syr, too?"

Lyu followed up, curious about the sudden announcement.

"What kind of errand?"

"A new hire like you thinks she needs an explanation for everything...You're awfully *overprotective* of this stupid girl."

Me? Overprotective of Syr?

Completely confused, Lyu shifted her gaze to Syr, who just smiled wryly. When she tried to ask again, Mia waved her off, not in the mood to pay it any mind.

"Jeez, this stupid girl is way more annoying than you...Maybe I should just throw her out."

"Mama Mia~, I didn't do anything~!"

Mia looked extremely annoyed as the girl pretended to cry. Lyu was just perplexed, unable to follow the semblance of a conversation.

"Well, because of that, I'm counting on you to take care of things. Let the others know, too."

"...Understood."

"Incidentally, this has nothing to do with what we were just talking about, but don't go breaking anything in the bar. After I come back, if anything has happened to my place...you'll pay for it."

More ludicrous demands...

As the dwarf leaned in with a threatening expression, Lyu subconsciously pursed her lips and nodded.

"I'll remember that."

Evening.

Mia and Syr left the tavern, and Ahnya and the rest threw their aprons over their heads and cheered in celebration. The staff, which was usually oppressed by heavy labor, gladly welcomed the unexpected time off.

They cheered so much that Lyu found herself thinking, *Are you that excited?* And of course, it was pointless for Lyu to try to stop them.

While Mia was away, a small party began in the side building's dinner hall, everyone eating and drinking what they wanted. The catgirl Mei made all of the tavern's signature dishes and lined them up on the table. It looked so good that even the conscientious elf reached out and took some against her better judgment. The next day, the mistress's wrath was sure to strike.

Several girls became drunk and were sleeping together in a huddle in the dining hall.

Of the dozens of employees, Lyu was the only sober one. She gave up on carrying them to their individual rooms and just spread blankets over them.

She returned to her own room, sighing and smiling as she remembered getting up to similar antics while she was in *Astrea Familia*.

Moonlight shone through the window.

In the side building, Lyu had been allocated a single room. There was no vestibule and no furniture, except for a bed and a table. In the corner was a knapsack with her weapons and tools stuffed into it.

When she lay down, Lyu was soon wrapped in a peaceful drowsiness. She had the adventurer's habit of sleeping lightly while still maintaining some degree of alertness, but for some reason, tonight she felt comfortable.

In that case, she would be able to make it until *that time* without opening her eyes.

A sweet fragrance invited Lyu even deeper into sleep—

"—!"

In an instant, she was awake again.

She wrenched open her eyes as she shook off her drowsiness. She pinched her cheek and held her arm up to her nose.

"This smell…Sleeping Scent!"

It was an item that put anyone who inhaled it to sleep. Depending on the ingredients and how it was made, it was possible to make a normal person sleep so deeply that practically nothing could wake them up.

It had been so strong that she had almost slept despite her well-developed Resistance, which made Lyu shudder. A skilled herbalist—someone with a built-up Synthesis ability—had undoubtedly used the best ingredients to make this. She could guess it had cost a lot of money.

Even now, her head was still fuzzy, making it hard to think.

"Tch—!"

She shook her head to maintain her consciousness. *Don't stop moving. If I stop…*Lyu took out the two shortswords she had hidden under her pillow.

This can't be natural…An enemy attack!

There was no need to think further than that. Without a doubt, the target was Lyu.

Pursuers had come. An assassin to take out Gale Wind.

The enemy must have observed that The Benevolent Mistress employed many highly skilled people, so they would not have gone about it that simply; at the very least, they would not straight-up attack the tavern……After forming a hypothesis, Lyu cursed her carelessness.

They only want me…but I'm worried about Ahnya and the rest.

The Sleeping Scent had probably permeated the three-story building. Other than Lyu, every other staff member would have fallen completely asleep and would not be able to wake up. Fearing the possibility of hostages, Lyu moved immediately.

Stopping only to quickly put on her boots, she approached the room's wooden door.

—There.

Grasping the knob with her fingers, Lyu could feel it. Some shadowy existence shrouded in the dark night had come down the hall and was just on the other side. Holding her breath, she turned the doorknob.

Giii…! A creaking sound rang out as Lyu opened the door.

"…?"

As she entered the hallway, she looked around, but there was only stillness. She could not see any suspicious shadows. The only light source in the hall was the pale gleam of the stars through the window.

The wooden hallway returned to silence.

—Nothing?

Lyu doubted her instincts, but the next instant…

"——"

A shadow stuck to the ceiling dropped down without a noise.

Shining in the darkness was a pair of green cat eyes.

Their owner was holding a sharp assassin's dagger. The claws of the figure's left hand let go of the wooden slats, and it kicked off the ground.

A strong attack came from Lyu's blind spot.

"—?!"

Instinctively, Lyu jumped to the side with a grunt. As she moved, she just barely dodged the surprise attack.

Zan! The blade of the knife stabbed into the floor as Lyu's roll kicked up some dust.

"A-ah…!"

A bead of sweat flew as Lyu quickly righted herself. The shadow in front of her stood up in a slow, graceful motion.

A black hood pulled low over her eyes, battle clothes that emphasized ease of movement, high-laced boots.

The small assassin smiled, her slender tail wriggling back and forth, and her cat ears making two mounds in her hood.

"It would have ended more easily for you if you were asleep."

Lyu eyed the sharp assassin's blade in her right hand as she drew in her breath and spoke.

"You're…Black Cat?"

The assassin only responded with an elusive smile. Hidden behind her hood, she sighed ever so slightly.

"The assassination was a failure…"

She gently released the weapon she was holding. In accordance with the laws of nature, the knife dropped. Just as Lyu was caught off guard by the odd movement—Black Cat kicked the knife.

"Guh!"

"Now I'm coming with brute force."

Lyu dodged the knife flying at her. In that opening, Black Cat took a smoke ball out of her breast pocket and threw it to the floor. A smoke screen.

"Frolic."

Using the smoke as a distraction, she chanted softly.

An incantation!

Lyu only just made out a spell. It was most likely an extremely short-triggered chant.

What's coming?

Her field of vision constrained, Lyu's tension increased dramatically. In a hall too narrow to be a proper battlefield, she immediately readied her swords.

"——Guh!"

From behind.

Betraying Lyu's expectation, Black Cat charged. Hidden in the smoke, she sliced from behind. Shocked her opponent had caught her unawares from behind, Lyu responded with her shortswords, Futaba.

But…

"What?!"

The blade she swung with her left hand hit only air. The blade sliced through her enemy's torso with no feedback—Black Cat's figure disappeared like a haze of fog.

"An illusion?!"

What scattered instead of blood were particles of light called mana.

As her eyes widened, the black shadow again aimed at her back.

"Correct."

Her opponent whispered, her lips curved enchantingly. It was illusionary magic to confuse her enemy. This time, the real Black Cat flashed a high-speed thrust.

"Whoa!"

Lyu responded to the unexpected attack with whirlwind-like force. Her right hand swung so fast her body blurred as she turned around and deflected the fatal attack aimed at her back.

"!!"

A loud metallic sound rang out. Sparks lit both of their faces to reveal Lyu's strained profile and the shocked expression on Black Cat's lips below her hood. Having survived the attack, they immediately put some distance between them.

"You could block that…I really hate Level Fours. I even used my trump card."

"Tch…!"

"But *I cut you.*"

Barely visible in the smoke, Black Cat showed her the blood residue that indicated her knife had hit.

The enemy's weapon, the blade was dyed a light purple.

Poison? Lyu guessed.

The small scratch on her right arm was giving off an abnormal amount of heat, confirming her suspicions.

"This one is called Violator. It's cute, right? This is my special tool. I have it absorb lots and lots of poison."

"...!"

"What it absorbed today was...Liquid Poison Vermis."

Lyu's face twisted as she heard the name of a certain valuable drop item. An intense toxin so strong that even a couple drops could make a top-tier adventurer suffer, even if they had Resistance. And of course, it would be deadly if left untreated.

"You don't have the special antidote, right? Well, not that I'd let you use it even if you did."

From behind Black Cat, another illusion appeared, giggling. Sleeping Scent, poison, illusion.

I see. Just like the rumors—an abundance of attacks aiming for weak spots. Between all of that and an agility that made Lyu break out into a cold sweat, she was sure this was Black Cat. The assassin whose name resounded loudest in Orario's underworld.

"...You were hired...to come kill me, huh?"

"Yes. The payment is the reward on your head, though."

"The person who hired you?"

"You think I'll tell you?"

As Lyu started to sweat from the intense poison eating away at her, Black Cat smiled scornfully.

The combination of the smoke curtain and the enemy's illusion was brutal. It was near impossible to find her real body, with only the faintest footsteps separating the two.

She had to escape the smoke-filled corridor. But of course, the enemy also recognized that and had surely strung out traps—her Strategy.

Smiling coldly, Black Cat, along with her illusion, disappeared into the smoke. She chanted "*Frolic!*" again. This time she intended to end it.

—I have to get out of the enemy's assassination range.

Bracing herself for a few wounds, the instant Lyu pressed her boots into the floor…

"Hi, I'm butting in."

Outside the window, a shadow danced.

"——"

The moment Lyu and Black Cat heard that voice in their ears, a fist swung down from the shadows. Immediately after, the window frame *shattered.*

"Uuuuh!"

"Unyah!"

Though Lyu had immediately taken evasive action, the force tossed her into the air as the the cat wrapped in a curtain of smoke cried out. Countless fragments scattered as the wooden floor collapsed.

Lyu gave up trying to understand the situation and chose to retreat instead. In the back of the tavern, there was an area set aside for another planned building—the inner courtyard where she landed.

"…The side building…"

Raising her head, Lyu lost her voice at the scene above her. On the three-story building, one hallway…was gone, as if it had been blown to smithereens.

"…How am I going to explain this to Mama Mia?"

The first thing that came to mind was the ogre-like expression Mia would make. Covered in cold sweat, the elf immediately shook her head.

Chasing away stupid distractions, she looked out over the destruction.

"Magic…No…Could that have been bare hands?"

Thinking back to the voice she heard just before the explosion, Lyu had a terrifying thought.

They probably jumped from a nearby building and approached the side building. And put all of their strength into their fist.

Finally, a shadow slid out of the hallway where the remnants of the smoke screen were dissipating and landed in the courtyard where Lyu was standing.

"I guess this really won't be easy, huh…? Well, surprise attacks don't really sit well with me, so it's okay, I guess."

A scarf wrapped around her neck, her shoulders and chest covered by lightweight clothes, and leather fingerless gloves on her fists, a human girl stood before Lyu, her chestnut-colored hair fluttering.

"Wh-what are you doing meow? *Cough!* Why are you here, all of a sudden! Are you really Black Fist?!"

"Oh, yeah. Aren't you Black Cat? Then it's a double bounty!"

In the dense smoke of the hallway, a dust-covered Black Cat screamed out. The human who was being shouted at looked up and disinterestedly responded.

"When two people have the same target, the faster one wins—that's my rule. No grudge over who gets her first."

"Eei! A muscle-brain, just like the rumors…"

As Black Cat spat in frustration, the girl turned to Lyu.

"That being the case, I'm going to kill you now."

"…Even Black Fist is after me…"

Standing before Black Fist, a bounty hunter whose fame matched Black Cat's, Lyu felt out of place more than scared.

The assassin aside, being followed by a bounty hunter drove it home that people really did want her dead.

At the same time, Lyu felt a sense of wonder, realizing that both Black Fist's and Black Cat's appearances and behaviors were those of girls a similar age to hers.

"Get ready. I don't really like fighting people who don't know what's coming."

"…"

Lyu took her stance as Black Fist hit her fists together, preparing for war.

Figuring out an escape is pointless, since I probably can't avoid a fight anymore. But unlike Black Cat, she is straightforward and by the book.

A speech like that did not really suit a bounty hunter.

A three-way fight with Black Fist and Black Cat...can I hold out?

She examined her body as sweat glistened on her skin, the poison already working its way through her system.

"Orraah!"

"!!"

They charged together, trading punches and slashes. Weaving together dodges and counters, they kept switching places as a dizzying display of offense and defense unfolded in the blink of an eye. Lyu's outline blurred as her blade sang through the air.

Black Fist's—Runoa's—body pitched about as she unleashed a storm of blows.

Befitting her name, she did not target any weak spots like Black Cat. It was just a straightforward brawling match.

Using both of her fists in a bare-knuckle brawl—just straight-up hand-to-hand.

She's faster!

Runoa clicked her tongue at her opponent's Agility.

Her strength is higher.

Lyu scrutinized her opponent's Strength.

"""!!"""

One deflected swords; the other parried fists. The flash of a blade sent blood spurting from a cheek; a barely dodged punch ripped part of a tunic. As the evenly matched battle unfolded, Lyu and Runoa's battle for supremacy sped up.

"Muscle-brained freaks are nice and simple, meow."

As Lyu and Runoa violently battled, Black Cat—Chloe—looked down from the top of the building she had climbed. She left the hot-blooded fools to themselves. Aiming to profit from their struggle, Chloe laughed derisively, waiting for Gale Wind and Black Fist to wear themselves out.

"They probably both expect me to intervene...but it's hopeless, meow. I'll just keep attacking from the outside and sweep when the going gets good, meow."

A nasty smile on her face, she took out three throwing knives and held them between her fingers.

Other than the three combatants, no one would intervene. The people in neighboring buildings could surely hear the struggle and sounds of fighting, but they would prioritize avoiding trouble, accustomed as they were to brawls between ruffians. By the time the Guild and other adventurers hurried out, Gale Wind would already be dead.

It was the same for Gale Wind's coworkers. They were surely still deep in dreamland at this point thanks to the Sleeping Scent Chloe used.

There was no one to intervene. Chloe smiled from her unrivaled perch. Or so she thought.

"Fuwaa~ahh!"

"?!"

She spun around in shock at hearing a stupid-sounding yawn from behind her back.

"Mmmmeow...Something was kind of annoying and it woke me up, meow."

A girl with brown fur emerged on the rooftop, a catgirl like her. She was one of the staff at The Benevolent Mistress.

That stupid-looking catgirl. The one that spent so much time with Gale Wind, like that platinum-haired girl.

If I recall, her name is Ahnya.

Chloe was dumbfounded.

"That's...! The scent's effect should have kept you from waking up for several hours—do I smell alcohol?!"

"Uuuuh~! I drank a little too much, mmmeow..."

The stench of alcohol wafted over as Chloe covered her nose instinctively. She recognized what had happened.

It's not that this catgirl was unaffected by the scent like the other staff. She was already asleep before the scent, and the sound of the hallway exploding and the fight finally woke her up. In other words—she's just an idiot!

"So you guys...are having some kind of showdown. Are you enemies of Lyu, meow?"

Though she was still half-asleep, Ahnya's eyes sharply narrowed in an instant. Chloe stared dumbly as a wave of tension built inside her.

Putting aside her stupidity and whatever else, she must have a Resistance on par with Gale Wind's to have overcome the sleeping scent. She's pretty capable for a restaurant worker.

Chloe found it suspicious that she had come to the roof instead of going over to Lyu. She could not tell whether she was insightful or just an idiot.

She had come holding something in her hand: a long, pole-shaped club wrapped in white cloth.

"…And if I am?"

Putting on a bold smile again, Chloe grabbed the assassin's blade Violator in one hand.

"I'll blow you away, meow!"

Ahnya launched herself forward. Chloe threw all the knives she had pulled out before as her opponent came at her head-on. Without waiting to see whether they had been deflected by the thing Ahnya was wielding, she threw a smoke bomb to her feet like before.

"*—Frolic!*"

Without a moment's delay, she chanted. As smoke shrouded Chloe, light particles swirled to her left and right.

"*Felis Kurus!*"

In an instant, two illusions appeared soundlessly.

Felis Kurus. An illusionary short-trigger magic that gave birth to mirages that were mirror images of the caster. The upper limit was two bodies. Without a real body, the mirages could not attack or defend, they just moved under Chloe's command. Chloe used this magic for confusion, disturbance, and surprise—all sorts of tricks useful for assassinations.

Hem her in, meow! Before she figures out they're mirages, stab her back!

For Chloe, who was bad at head-on fights, this was her method for a guaranteed victory. Distract Ahnya with the smoke curtain and surround her with mirages dancing all around her.

"I can't see anything, meow!"

Chloe licked her lips as Ahnya froze. However.

"This is annoying—meow!"

She was dumbfounded again as the girl used her weapon to kick up a whirlwind.

"Haaa!"

Taking a stance, she spun once with her weapon. The club mowed down both mirages and dispersed them in one blow before she returned to face Chloe, who instinctively began an emergency retreat. She was unable to dodge a strong hit to her shoulder that knocked her away.

"Meoww!"

With that, she was sent flying toward the courtyard where Lyu and Black Fist were fighting.

"What?! You're a catgirl, too, meow?"

Having blown away the smoke screen, Ahnya jumped down, too, landing right in front of Chloe.

Now that her hood was gone, Chloe stared in annoyance at her opponent.

The hallway had been narrow, but the rooftop was wide open; plus, the reach of Ahnya's weapon made her a very different opponent from Lyu. As did her wholehearted stupidity.

"Dammit, you just keep…!"

"Isn't it hard talking like that, even with another catgirl, meow? Don't try to act, just be yourself, meow!"

Crick! Something snapped in Chloe.

"Nuuuaa——You're talking pretty high and mighty, meow! Aren't you getting in the way of my greatness?"

"Oh, she talked, meow! And you even smell a little like me, meow!"

"Don't confuse me with an idiot, meow!"

"Who's an idiot, meow?"

Lyu and Runoa glanced over in annoyance at the yowling cat pair.

"I know, meow! This is like that doppelganger thing, meow!"

"Who's a doppelganger, meow? Look closer, meow, my body and tail are more slender. I'm a *cool beauty*, meow!"

"But my breasts are bigger, meow!"

"Y-you…!"

Ahnya put her hands on her waist and thrust out her chest in pride as Chloe's voltage skyrocketed.

"Oh…it tore. Guess I'll take it off, meow."

Ahnya removed the white cloth wrapped around her club weapon. What emerged was a masterfully crafted spear. Chloe's eyes opened wide.

"An engraved golden long spear…It couldn't be."

She had heard of it before. In a certain *Goddess of Beauty's large faction*, there was a silver spear–wielding cat-person adventurer who was called "the fastest." That adventurer had a younger sister. She had disappeared from the main stage at some point: a golden spear wielder. Her other name was…

"You…Vana Alfi?!"

"It's been a long time since I've heard that name, meow…"

Ahnya's ears seemed to droop sadly at Chloe's words. But that was just for a split second. Pulling herself together, Ahnya put on a cheerful smile.

"Right now, I'm just the stray cat Ahnya. I don't know anything about Vana Alfi, meow."

She spun her spear and prepared herself.

"Time to blow you away real quick and go help Lyu, meow."

"Tch…Just you try, meow!"

Glaring at each other, they sprinted. The knife and spear flashed as the two catgirls collided.

"…!"

As Lyu dodged the barrage of punches by the skin of her teeth, another bead of sweat splashed from her skin.

"Orrrah! How about this?"

Runoa resolutely attacked, her scarf dancing as she moved.

She's strong…

Runoa's—Black Fist's—true strength was greater than Lyu had imagined. Her self-taught style of attack was ferocious, and the force behind each punch was tremendous. When she hit the ground, the paving stones shattered, leaving craters. She had that much force without using enchantment—her stats in that area were superior.

Just as her alias indicated, despite using only her fists, her storm of wild hits did not give Lyu the time to counterattack.

It's the poison…No, even if I were at full strength…!

Lyu was fighting a defensive struggle, racked by the pain emanating from her right arm where the assassin's blade had nicked her. Even accounting for that, Black Fist's attacks would have been difficult to manage.

She restricted her enemy's paths to escape using her natural genius for brawling and raw instincts. The gloves she wore had plates installed across the back of the hand to aid in dealing with swords, so even when Lyu thrust her swords in desperation, they were parried.

Finally, Runoa's fist landed cleanly on Lyu's chest.

"Guh?!"

She reflexively jumped back as she was pummeled by an unthinkable blow. Her internal organs were wounded, and she coughed up some blood as she hit the ground hard.

She rolled to the side as a tightly clenched fist landed for an immediate follow-up attack; the stone flooring shattered behind her.

—I have no choice…

This was not the time to be holding back. Standing up and wiping the blood away, she resolved herself. She opened her mouth as she continued trading blows with the girl rushing in:

"*—Distant forest sky. Infinite stars inlaid in the eternal night sky.*"

"Concurrent Casting?!"

Runoa's eyes went wide as the chant began before her.

She's trying to use magic? I'll wait and see…

The high-speed casting was unleashing enough magic to make her opponent tense up. Not only did they not know the nature of the spell, but they also had to be wary of the chance it was a sure-kill trump card. The prudent choice for Runoa would be to switch to a hit-and-run strategy—

—As if!!

But she did not.

"Orraaaaa!!"

"?!"

Far from it, she increased her attacks on Lyu by another level. Her opponent's sky-blue eyes clouded in distress.

It's a bluff, I'm not falling for it!

She read Lyu's aim.

She was pretending to bring in the big guns in order to get her opponent to fall back and find a chance for attack or else try snatching an opening to disappear. With that much magic in front of them, even an upper-class adventurer would get impatient and mess up their strength and rhythm. It was a tactic commonly used by magic swordsfighters.

However, Runoa was unperturbed.

Runoa's strongest trait was not the force behind her fists but strategy. Just by herself, living only on her own strength, even in Orario her nerves were a cut above the rest.

Corner yourself with Ignis Fatuus—!

Concurrent Casting is amazing, but it's a bad choice for fighting me.

With that much magical energy, once she lost control of it, Lyu would destroy herself from the inside from the blowback.

Runoa had finished off countless magic swordsmen in dramatic close-range fights like this.

Runoa howled, showing what she was worth without any fear.

"Blow yourself up and drop dead!"

She wound up even higher, unleashing more and more punches.

"*—Heed this foolish one's voice, and once more grant the starfire's divine protection.*"

However, Lyu kept chanting.

"——"

"*Grant the light of compassion to the one who forsook you.*"

As Runoa went wide-eyed, Lyu continued to weave her spell without faltering or slowing down. She kept chanting without stopping, sweat flying as fists grazed her, like a singing, dancing fairy. Far from stopping, she sped up.

This elf...did she really—

Runoa realized she had *misread* her. Lyu had recognized she would move in to try to stop her and intended to ride out her Concurrent Casting.

Attack, defense, movement, evasion, and chanting—she did all five at once. She had an unabated, overwhelming battle speed that far exceeded what Runoa had imagined. She continued to chant at the front lines of the battle, putting out everything she had.

It was not a bluff or anything of the sort.

This elf believed in herself. Her Technique, her experience overcoming countless scenes of carnage.

The strength of magic had saved herself and her comrades in the abyss of the Dungeon, which Runoa had never seen.

"*Come, wandering wind, fellow traveler.*"

A single misstep would be self-destruction. If she took a hit from Runoa, she would be pulverized. As if unconcerned by any of that, Lyu's chanting voice did not waver at all.

A will of steel, or rather "the spirit of the great tree."

Lyu had nerves to rival the great holy tree said to be raised in the elven forest—Runoa's heart trembled at a foolhardiness that exceeded than her own. She did not have any way to get out of range of the magic anymore.

This is bad—!

Sweat poured out of her body.

"*Cross the skies and sprint through the wilderness, swifter than anything. Imbue the light of stardust and strike down my enemy!*"

Lyu did not overlook her hesitation. She completed the chant in one swoop.

She activated it instantly.

"*Luminous Wind!!*"

A giant ball of light shrouded in a green wind burst forth with a flash.

""""~~~~~~~""""

Lyu and Runoa were both blown back.

"Funyaa!"

"Hey, wa—Meowwwwwww!"

It also devoured Ahnya and Chloe nearby.

Lyu's tremendous attack sent all four girls flying. Several magical bullets flew around where Runoa and Lyu were fighting in the courtyard. All of the buildings nearby were covered in cracks, billows of smoke rising from the scene of destruction.

"Guh~~~~~! You were prepared to blow yourself up...You really did it...!"

"If you were farther away, I wouldn't have hit you..."

Runoa dragged herself out of the broken storage shed, a hateful smile on her face. Peeling herself off the wall of the side building, Lyu wiped her sweat- and burn-covered face. Lyu had not given Runoa the chance to dodge, unleashing her magical cannon at short range.

"You idiot, Lyu~~~~~~~~!! I came to help you! What are you doing, meow?!"

"Are you trying to kill us, meow?!"

"Ahnya aside, didn't you come here to assassinate me?"

As Ahnya and Chloe stood up from the wreckage, whining, Lyu looked at Chloe with half-closed eyes. She was about to apologize to Ahnya, but she stopped when Runoa approached.

"Ahhhh! Nice, I'm burning up! Idiots like you are why I could never quit this job."

Runoa laughed savagely as she punched her right fist into her left palm, true to her nature.

She knew it was imprudent, but in front of such a straightforward personality, Lyu broke into a smile as well.

She immediately fixed her expression and readied her twin blades.

"—Ha-ha-ha! This is perfect; you beat yourselves up!"

All of a sudden, a new voice rang out through the courtyard.

"...Huh?"

"This is..."

Runoa raised an eyebrow and Lyu looked around as a crowd of thugs emerged. They were holding swords and clubs in their hands.

"The Bruno Corporation…? What's all this? I told you to leave Gale Wind to me!"

Runoa fixed the human leading the thugs with a piercing glare. Next to him was a dwarf with a vile smile.

"That dwarf…he's the one who brought me this contract, meow!"

Chloe's eyes narrowed, as they all started to recognize what was happening.

"I see how it is…It wasn't just Gale Wind, it was us, from the beginning…"

"Correct! Black Fist and Black Cat—you two are also thorns in our side!"

The human merchant—one of the top brass of the Bruno Corporation—grinned.

"We had you two fight Gale Wind, so that we could take you out once you had been weakened…That was the real meaning of the contract! It was convenient that only our Bruno Corporation had Leon's information!"

In other words, the double bounty on Gale Wind was also part of their plan.

The two people who were secretly part of the same group used the same information in order to lure in Runoa and Chloe, working to get them both to eliminate Lyu on the same day.

"The Evils were defeated thanks to none other than you, Leon! After that, this town, Orario, was reborn!"

The merchant put to words the same future that several people had felt and then continued.

"And the one who will establish the order of the newly reborn Orario is our corporation!

"So now, we can't afford to leave disruptive elements like you two has-been, unaffiliated mercenaries!"

The mastermind ecstatically announced his plans.

Their eyes narrowed as they caught a glimpse of the merchant's greed as he gratified his own selfish desires.

"And most importantly, we can't allow people who know about our connection to the Evils to live! Do it, you guys!"

He thrust his hand out, ordering the throngs of men forward. Licking their lips at the wounded beauties in front of them, the net of thugs started closing in.

However.

"Hmph...pointless."

"Such a third-rate villain, meow..."

Runoa and Chloe sighed deeply after this disheartening revelation, losing their drive.

"I'm most mad about being used for such a pointless plan..."

"It was unavoidable, meow. I was already worrying about retiring after this, meow..."

As they looked into the distance, Ahnya talked to Lyu.

"Hey, Lyu? Is it okay to blow them away, meow?"

"I don't mind. There's no reason to hesitate."

The next instant, the thugs dove in to attack. Heaving a weary sigh, Runoa raised her head and spoke for everyone.

"—If you want to bring us down, then you better come with at least ten times this many."

Immediately after, there was a chain reaction of screams. In an instant, the agonizing cries rising into the starry sky were cut off, and the mob of thugs were viciously beaten and splayed across the courtyard.

It was an easy victory.

"Wh-whaaaa...?!"

"Ten times, my ass! Even twenty times wouldn't be enough, meow!"

While kicking the human and the dwarf client, Chloe laughed sadistically. The merchant was beaten until his face was disfigured, his lips opening and closing like a fish.

"D-don't think you've seen the last of us...! Our Bruno Corporation lurks in the shadows...!"

"Ah, you're annoying. Shut up already."

A fist swung down, and a squelched whimper followed.

The masterminds pulling the strings behind this violence were easily wiped out. The only ones left standing in the end were the same as at the start: the four girls.

"Shall we continue?"

"Obviously. Just had to take care of a little business first."

"Bring it, meow!"

"I'll beat you to death, meow!"

Runoa, Lyu, Ahnya, and Chloe exchanged sharp gazes. Their heads hot with fervor, they prepared to start fighting again.

"Let's go!"

However—

Thud, thud...

As they took their stances, they heard the earth trembling.

"This sound is..."

"What, meow...?"

"........."

"........."

Runoa and Chloe were confused.

Ahnya turned ghostly pale, while Lyu started sweating anew, and not because of the poison.

Finally, the source of the trembling earth appeared before their eyes with a shout of rage.

"—Oi, dumbasses!"

It was Mia.

"What is this?"

The window and hallway of the side building were blown away, and the storage shed and alcohol warehouse had a big hole in them with food and bottles in disarray. The carnage covered the carefully set-aside area that had been planned for a new building.

It was laughably battered.

"Whose bar is this? Huh? Answer me."

The owner of The Benevolent Mistress had returned. A waterfall of sweat started flowing down Lyu's brow. Sensing that this was not just some random shop owner, Runoa and Chloe stood stock-still. Ahnya was wracked with sobs as tears welled up in her eyes. Mia's face was downcast in the darkness, so they could not tell what she was looking at.

"Mama! Mei and the girls got drunk on the alcohol——......... Ah-ha-ha-ha! It's probably better not to say that..."

As Syr came running over, she saw Mia and then Lyu and the rest after she had already started speaking. Seeing the situation, she forced a laugh before she ran away by herself.

No help was coming.

"M-Mama, Mama! Hear me out, meow! There's a good excuse—!"

Ahnya ran over to Mia, unable to hold out. *Kabam!!!!* The cat-girl who came before her, desperately trying to explain, sank to the ground after a single blow from the giant dwarf.

"————————"

The other three were at a loss for words as Ahnya lay facedown, smoke rising from the top of her head. The earth trembled again as the giant dwarf moved in front of the frozen girls.

Standing in her shadow, Lyu knew the feeling she had when they first met was correct. She had thought she had just mistaken her for someone else, but she had not.

Beautiful and lovely. A certain adventurer with the same name. She looked nothing like the rumors, so Lyu had not believed it. Her lips trembled now that she knew for sure.

"Mia...Mia Grand."

"That's...*Freya Familia*'s *former head.*"

"Level Six...Demi Ymir, the little giant."

Runoa and Chloe turned pale as they murmured. Their bodies knew it. Or rather, they remembered...

In Orario—there were monsters beyond imagining.

"You—"

The dwarf looked up with a dreadful expression and released all of her fury:

"—dumbasseeeeeeeeessssssssss!"

5

Warm morning sun poured down.

A clear, cloudless blue sky announced the beginning a brisk new day. The clamor of people on Main Street was peaceful.

"Uuuhh…why am I doing this kind of thing, meow…?"

"You're annoying. Just shut up and work, stupid cat…"

On that peaceful morning, a couple of people choked back tears as they worked. Chloe and Runoa.

They were wearing waitress outfits—the uniform of The Benevolent Mistress. They were nailing boards to the broken-down parts of the side building and storage shed.

"It's because you guys busted up the shop, meow…"

"The one who broke the building wasn't me, meow! It was this muscle-brained bounty hunter and that homicidal elf, meow!"

"Wait, don't go blaming other people, stupid cat!"

"I always go too far…"

Along with Chloe and Runoa, Ahnya was removing rubble, and Lyu was pulling the wheelbarrow it was loaded into.

It was three days after the incident.

Having suffered Mia's imperial wrath, they were forced to do the cleanup work for the destroyed areas around the tavern, working until today. As indicated by their outfits, Chloe and Runoa were The Benevolent Mistress's newest employees.

The careers of Black Fist and Black Cat, terrors of the underworld, had ended with a whimper.

"I'm going to escape. I'll definitely escape, meow…!"

"That's a bad idea, giving up is better..."

"Mama's special distilled fruit wine. When the storehouse was blown to pieces, it went bad, meow..."

Chloe swore she would escape as she swung her hammer with teary eyes, but Lyu and Ahnya had knowing looks. Chloe and Runoa had smashed up Mia's property. They were ordered to work until they had paid back what they owned. The amount specified was 100 million valis.

"It's just some booze and an old building, that's absurd, meow!" "Yeah, yeah!" They had tried to argue, but they were laid flat with a single blow from Mia's clenched fist. Trying to plead their case with the dwarf they had enraged was hopeless.

—Incidentally, the catgirls who had started a party by themselves were even now working triple shifts in the tavern to dry up.

The open area that had been planned for another building had been damaged too much, so it was now being turned into a courtyard.

"But I think this is good, meow. Thanks to Mama, the guys who knew your identity were caught by the Guild, so now no one will come after you, meow?"

"Probably, although this isn't good at all. In the end, that crazy dwarf is the one controlling my fate!"

The black-and-blue head of the Bruno Corporation who had tried to take down Gale Wind, Black Fist, and Black Cat had been taken to the Guild on that day. They took that opportunity to round up *the entire Bruno Corporation*, too. All of it was Mia's work.

She had not been satisfied with simply dealing with the girls who had busted up her tavern.

"If you say anything about these girls, *I'll bury you.* If you leak anything to the Guild, *I'll bury you.* Whatever I do, *I will bury you.*"

Looking furious as she lightly tied them up, that faction of the Bruno Corporation literally started foaming at the mouth. Five years later, she would make a heroic march into the corporation and single-handedly destroy the familia-scale organization that hid behind the scenes—.

After that trauma was impressed upon them, the names of the wanted people never crossed their lips ever again.

"Quit chattering, you stupid girls!"

Mia's angry shout rang out from the direction of the tavern, sending shivers down their spines.

Seeing them freeze in terror, Lyu averted her eyes, knowing this involved her, too.

What happened that night…I don't ever want to remember it.

"Everyone, breakfast!"

"Hurray, meow!"

"We've been at it since early, so I'm starving…"

Chloe and Runoa cheered when Syr came to the courtyard to call them, and the four girls started to move.

"Ahh, at this point the only reason to keep living is the food, meow…"

"Ah, this is bad. We're in such deep trouble…"

"According to the owner, eating delicious food is reason enough to live."

"That know-it-all face is so annoying, meow!"

"Yeah, yeah, this useless elf!"

"What? Correct yourself! I'm not useless!"

"Mya-ha-ha-ha! Lyu is definitely useless, meow!…Meow? Idiot or useless…which is better, meow?"

"You're super-dumb *and* annoying, so just shut up, meow!"

"What'd you say?!"

"Everyone's getting along well, it seems."

"""""Not at all!"""""

Syr seemed to be smiling as they responded in unison. She started giggling and then turned toward Runoa and Chloe.

"Also, you have guests, Runoa and Chloe."

"Us?"

"Meow?"

As they followed Syr to the entrance of the tavern—

"Congratulations on your new job~!"

"You surprised me. Who'd have thought you'd be working at a tavern."

"Demeter?!"

"And Njörðr, meow?!"

The cheerful goddess and congenial god had come bearing produce and seafood.

"I heard from Syr that there were new workers, so I wondered if it might be..."

"When I heard the description, it was dead on. Here, a celebratory gift."

"De-Demeter, you've got it wrong!"

"We aren't staff, meow! We're slaves! Slaves, meow!"

Njörðr and Demeter smiled broadly as they watched Chloe and Runoa struggling to explain.

"But it's a relief. You've gotten used to it and all."

"You've put on various facades, but you look much livelier than before."

Runoa and Chloe were at a loss for words as the gods looked at them with kind eyes, as if watching over children. They glanced at each other with an uneasy, dissatisfied sort of look.

"We're a lot alike, meow! And we get along perfectly, meow!"

"Don't lump me with an idiot like you, meow!"

"Well, it's probably fine not to worry...That is, there's no need to."

"Yes, I agree."

Ahnya jumped in with a misplaced sense of pride and Chloe snapped back instantly as Runoa and Lyu nodded in agreement.

As a result of their gigantic fight to the death, or perhaps just a brawl between them, they had become coworkers who could argue and trade fists without concern. Chloe and Runoa were certainly smiling at that point.

Seeing that, Demeter and Njörðr both grinned.

"Next time I'll bring Persephone and the rest. We'll enjoy the food you bring us."

"Okay...Thank you very much for everything up until now, Demeter."

"Looks like you got some companions finally. You said you couldn't make friends, but you've got a place where you belong. Treasure it."

"Njörðr, I'm sorry for all the trouble I caused, meow...Thank you."

The way the girls said their thanks and accepted the gods' gifts was reminiscent of the bonds between deities and their followers.

Demeter and Runoa hugged. Chloe's tail trembled as Njörðr patted her head, announcing the end of their relationship. The girls smiled until it was over.

"—Recently, we've had more employees loafing about, so this is a good opportunity. Gather 'round."

After the gods had left and breakfast was over, Mia assembled the staff of the tavern. Crowded among the chairs and tables, they focused on the mistress standing behind the counter.

"I'm the law in this shop. I'm the owner. Whatever I say is absolute. Even gods don't quibble with me."

"She's really not scared of the gods at all, meow..."

Chloe whispered absentmindedly as Mia crossed her arms and looked cocky.

"And since I'm the owner, I'm your Mama. You all are my girls. Everything in this bar in mine, and anyone who tries to lay a hand on anything of mine will pay for it."

Lyu, Runoa, and Chloe all went wide-eyed. Syr and Ahnya and the rest, who had been at the tavern longer, smiled.

This was The Benevolent Mistress.

The tavern that could send any strong adventurer, outlaw, or villain running away in fear.

And no matter what their past, girls would be worked like mules, serving delicious food and alcohol, sharing smiles with lots of guests—a benevolent restaurant.

"Got it, you stupid new girls? Starting today, you call me Mama!"

This time she looked directly at Lyu, Runoa, and Chloe. One groaned, another was embarrassed, and the third made a face of disgust, but the scolding voice prodded them.

"Quickly, now!"

"...Mama Mia."

"...Mama Mia."

Their cheeks red with embarrassment, Runoa and Chloe mumbled her name. Finally came Lyu.

"...Mama Mia."

She looked straight at the mistress, the words coming out without resistance—to her surprise.

For some reason she could not comprehend, she smiled. Smiling in acknowledgement, Mia nodded.

"Well, then, guests are coming! Raise your voices! Even at the shittiest of times, this is a place to come eat food with a smile."

Grinning, she gave a rousing shout. Obeying their mistress, the cute girls in uniform gathered by the front door.

They greeted the guests approaching with a smile, and said in unison:

"Welcome to The Benevolent Mistress! Come on in!"

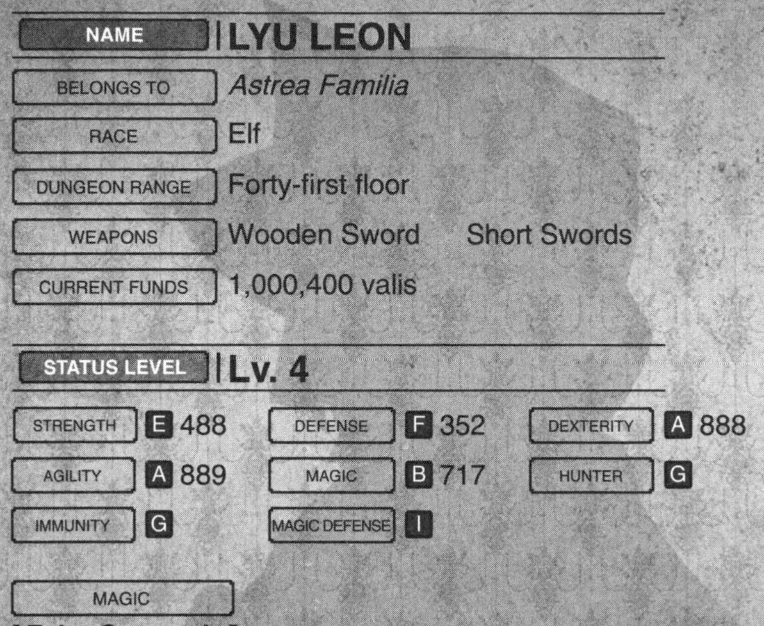

NAME	LYU LEON
BELONGS TO	*Astrea Familia*
RACE	Elf
DUNGEON RANGE	Forty-first floor
WEAPONS	Wooden Sword Short Swords
CURRENT FUNDS	1,000,400 valis

STATUS LEVEL	Lv. 4				
STRENGTH	E 488	DEFENSE	F 352	DEXTERITY	A 888
AGILITY	A 889	MAGIC	B 717	HUNTER	G
IMMUNITY	G	MAGIC DEFENSE	I		

MAGIC

【Fairy Serenade】

- Amplify magic effect.
- Improved enhancement at night.

【Mind Load】

- When attacking, consume Mind to increase Strength.
- Active Trigger. The amount of Mind consumed can be adjusted.

【Aero Mana】

- When sprinting, the faster the user goes, the greater their attack power.

ITEMS

《Alvs Lumina》

- Fashioned from a branch of the holy tree that grows in Lyu's birthplace, Lyumirua Forest.
- The branch was retrieved in a certain incident, then entrusted to *Goibniu Familia* to create an order-made weapon. Besides having high attack and stoutness, it can also amplify magic.
- The branch harmonizes particularly well with elf magic.

《Short Swords Futaba》

- Two short swords.
- A gift from a member of *Astrea Familia* who hailed from the Far East. With extraordinarily keen edges, they are considerably sharp swords even among tier-two weapons.
- The only item that Lyu did not return at her friends' grave.

LYU
LEON

AFTERWORD

This is the first installment of the newest series of *Is It Wrong to Try to Pick Up Girls in a Dungeon?*

In the end, I started another side story.

Personally, I would like this so-called "Chronicle" series to cover several characters. The top of the lineup was the elf at the tavern who is popular even in the main series, but I was thinking of changing the main character in the next book (of course, the batting order would cycle back around so that characters could get another book). I intend the Chronicle to touch more on the characters' pasts that I could not really delve into in the main series or side story.

I wanted the elf from the tavern featured in this book to be properly connected to the main series, but I was a bit unsure about how far I should portray it. After thinking about it a lot, I wrote "Crush the Grand Casino!" to take place in the period of time between books six and seven of the main series, and "That Is a Benevolent Tavern ~ Girl Meets Girls ~" about how the tavern girls with dark pasts met before the start of the main series. Gangan GA published the former in short story form, and the latter was written for this book.

Even though I made it, I particularly enjoyed the relationship between the bounty hunter and assassin. Starting with a setting that had a vague "their past probably is sort of like this" feel, as I was writing it, I surprised myself, thinking, "Huh, she was under that god at the time?" Several points I hadn't considered ended up connecting together as I kept writing. When things flow like that, it's best for the author to just accept it, and rediscovering pairings of unexpected characters is the charm of this series. Even setting aside the main and side series, the setting of this book moves smoothly, so I hope people will enjoy that, too.

Allow me to move on to the thanks.

My supervisor Mr. Kotaki, the editor Mr. Kitamura, everyone in

GA Bunko editing department, thanks for your help on this series. Thank you to the illustrator Mr. Niritsu for doing such a great job with the artwork, including the cover. I look forward to working with you again going forward! Also, my deepest thanks to everyone at Gangan GA and everyone involved who helped with the publication of this book. But most importantly, I'm grateful to all of the readers who picked this book up. Thank you very much. This has become a story with several concurrent series, so thank you for taking the time to join me.

From now on Gangan GA will publish these stories in short story form first.

I was thinking "If I could do a story about the beautiful goddess's followers…" for next time. Let's meet again next book.

Thank you for reading this far. Until next time,

Fujino Omori